pike and bloom

matthew nye

First published 2016 by &NOW Books, an
imprint of Lake Forest College Press.

Carnegie Hall
Lake Forest College
555 N. Sheridan Road
Lake Forest, IL 60045

lakeforest.edu/andnow

© 2016 Matthew Nye

Lake Forest College Press publishes in the broad spaces of
Chicago studies. Our imprint, &NOW Books, publishes
innovative and conceptual literature and serves as the publishing
arm of the &NOW writers' conference and organization.

ISBN: 978-1-941423-92-9

Library of Congress: 2015948226

Book and cover design by Rachel Tenuta

Cover image: Giovanni Battista Piranesi, *The
Gothic Arch*, from *Carceri d'invenzione* (*Imaginary
Prisons*), courtesy of metmuseum.org

Printed in the United States

LAKE FOREST
COLLEGE
PRESS

BOOKS

For Randy and Nancy

BOOK ONE

Pike gives himself advice, *cry, pounce, declare war*, and that did seem like a good idea, though not caring or never caring enough to do so, even a small war, and in a good climate, and without disease, hardship, clubfoot, and with well proportioned, well fitting, everything sparkling clean—peers with stark, strong, monosyllabic names—Mark, Luke, writers of the gospel—that when he ran scared and the doctor prodded his stomach, prodded his groin, fingers in white and teeth yellow, and the nurse who had no defining characteristics whatsoever, a Bradley Fighting Vehicle of a nurse said, "All of your organs appear to be working fine," he knew that she, the Bradley Nurse, was most definitively a terrible, terrible liar, not a nurse at all but like him a fraud, if a well-meaning fraud, and the doctor, his pulpy white fingers, bleeding into his core, where nothing is essentialized but packaged neatly in plastic, the doctor not a doctor, and Pike shouting to himself in his mind one-word imperatives and single-minded insulting profanities, does nothing, his stomach bare.

The White Fingered Doctor tells him that he has an "appendicitis," though not with very much conviction, and certainly not to be believed, a tone with raised eyebrows, perhaps not false but most certainly much dirtier—the tube-shaped sac at the end of his large intestine inflamed and angry, and after lying dormant for forty-odd years in Indianapolis, has decided now, on a Tuesday, to imminently burst. Why would it *decide* to do that? Pike thinks— though the White Fingered Doctor cautions him that it is perhaps not best to think of his appendix as making "conscious decisions," that it was in all likelihood an infection, a bacteria, an outside cause, and that they should "move quickly," the White Fingered Doctor says, in monotone and bored— the ceiling tiles all perfect 3x3 foot squares—and the Bradley Nurse again enters and takes him into another room exactly identical to the first.

He is wheeled down the canary-yellow hall-way and into the second room, a mode of travel that'll weaken one's self esteem, to be wheeled, and it weakens his, Pike's curious pride in being *able-bodied* now irrevocably turned—never fit exactly or athletic or strong, but *maintaining the minimum standard of*—and that was good, or good enough, not a real achievement, but real achieve-ments are hard to come by—fear, war, chronic fa-tigue—and being able-bodied had the upside of walking and climbing stairs, of turning the other way when frightened—though how much good was that really, Pike thinks, when depressed and complaining also having to accept cliché, the *at least you have your health*, and he didn't want to feel better but be affirmed in his pain, and he'd nod yes to privilege, to health, in spite of himself, he'd nod yes—but they can't say that now—let's see them try to say that now, and Pike feels a dry smile, finally justified in his calls to complain.

The White Fingered Doctor places a mask over his mouth and tells him to breathe. The White Fingered Doctor, a real Nat Turner, tells him about a news article in the *The New York Times* this morning and about its interview with Sixtus Petraeus—Pike on the operating table overhearing details about the procedure about to be performed, a request to the Bradley Nurse that the doctor's brow be wiped, that the patient's skin should be sterilized at the point of incision—and on the gurney he is fairly certain that Nat Turner is not to be trusted, certainly not trusted with a knife—and Sixtus Petraeus hearing in 1992 that his son David had been accidentally shot in the chest during a live-fire exercise was "not worried in the slightest." He knew that his son would be fine, that he could not be harmed by a mere shot to the chest, men of that quality, men of that character, and two weeks after the accident, David performs fifty push-ups at his hospital bedside, demanding to be placed back on active duty, in proof of his own combat readiness.

Waking in the first room, Pike is told that he
has been asleep for nearly forty hours and that
it is now Franz Mesmer Day, that he is watching *The Blue Angel* staring Marlene Dietrich on
the hospital television, and a nurse he does not
recognize says that he is not alone in having never heard of, or failing to observe, the holiday—a
quirk of the hospital patron, she says, who has
given generously, though very specifically, to Par-
kinson's research and advances in Mesmerism—
the good must go with the bad, she says—her
shoes also canary-yellow—the logical with the
mystical—and that growing up in Indianapolis, and its very serious blues, her father's father
would watch Marlene Dietrich films and attempt to hypnotize his wife for the purposes of
role play—that her grandmother would actually
believe that she was Marlene Dietrich and that
that belief made all the difference. The nurse gig-
gles and touches Pike's hand, and on the gurney,
his abdomen bandaged, *The Blue Angel* playing
on the hospital television, he knows that the
nurse is not to be trusted, that what she is telling
him is naive at best and the aftereffects of the
appendectomy at worst, the continuation of the
appendectomy, the fact that the White Fingered
Doctor had his hands inside him—and Marlene

Dietrich, as Lola, wears a black dress and looks right and then left—the glow from the television.

He is not terrified, Pike tells himself, but in control of all his faculties—extending his hand and brushing the blanket of the gurney, the accelerated beep of the heart monitor on edge, the mint of the toothpaste in his mouth—though Pike has no memory of brushing—and he knows that the Dietrich Nurse must have taken his teeth unconscious like a limp dog, lips slack and drooling—her canary-yellow shoes, the smell of her breath like gin and pineapple—the drink of choice of Lolita's Humbert—and what else has she done to him, he thinks—this morning alone in his Broad Ripple bungalow, all of his organs functioning properly, and like a time bomb set at forty-four years from birth, suddenly a crack in his appendix, the only organ he doesn't really use—not terrified, but rational, cogent, the thoughts of the surgically removed—and the White Fingered Doctor enters and places his hand on Pike's stomach as if he were a pregnant woman, the genuflection now to a void and a lack—and Marlene Dietrich is off the television and replaced by a young Tom Cruise—as a satyr or a puck staring eye to eye with a unicorn—and this is not comfortable—the hand on his stomach, the beep of the heart monitor—he picks out the word *success* from the White Fingered Doctor's speech, but what is being modified exactly, Pike thinks—Tom Cruise baring his bow and arrow.

The Dietrich Nurse comes and goes every two hours, her real tasks mixed with those certainly alternative—the documentation of his vital signs, the regular injections, and the social function of birthdays, to confirm that one is indeed still alive, accelerated artificially to two-hour intervals—looking over one's shoulders more often now for death—the constant interruptions, the squeak of canary shoes—and Pike is uncomfortable with the idea of those who are beautiful charged with life's dirty necessities, the maintenance of another, because the Dietrich Nurse is beautiful, if untrustworthy, if a Lola, and that kind of work is reserved for Solzhenitsyns in labor camps—not Marlene Dietrich, not Tom Cruise—a different kind of injustice, but one preserving the division of labor—authors from actors—and the television in his room cannot be turned off—the power button locked or broken—and Pike watches James Caan as rollerball champion Jonathan E. resist the calls for his retirement—he watches the Dietrich Nurse clean and care and wheel out dollies when patients expire.

In his room, sleep and wakefulness are functionally impossible—the interface of fluorescent bulb and dermis—the comings and goings of the Dietrich Nurse with Spandau-like clockwork—and the lights are always on, his eyelids not thick enough, a burning red when his eyes are closed—not the cool black conducive to sleep, nor the serious blues of Indianapolis. There are no windows in the room or views to the capital's towers—its Benjamin Harrison House, its Propylaeum, and Pike's own bungalow in the Broad Ripple district where they limit the circulation of his blood to the confines of his own body—where there are no artificial veins, tubes, electrical diodes—and the White Fingered Doctor has an ominous look—a curious sensibility—a way of saying *good day* that is patently inauthentic—and "good day" he says entering the room with the Bradley Nurse—the phantom sting of his lost appendix—and in good Cartesian fashion he is skeptical—the dream, the evil daemon—unclouded by the ontological argument—the White Fingered Doctor and his salutations—"You may leave tomorrow" the White Fingered Doctor says—"We're satisfied with your recovery"—"We should follow up in three-four weeks"—"It's been a pleasure Mr. Pike." "Good day."

There is something curious, Pike thinks, resisting the urge to panic—the White Fingered Doctor leaving with the Bradley Nurse—because surely the White Fingered Doctor is lying—surely it could not be this easy—Haussmann carving away the boulevards of Paris and how could he not panic—the dissection of disease, the sudden and immediate commodification of time—the Dietrich Nurse entering with another gurney and a smile—*tomorrow* the White Fingered Doctor had said—*tonight* perhaps, or *soon*—time now finite and limiting—mattering in some way in which it did not matter before—and the Dietrich Nurse places a syringe into his arm with a smile, and the new charge, a boy of roughly sixteen, takes his place on the bed adjacent to Pike's, and he reminds himself again not to panic—to be rational, to be clear—to consider the time and date, the schedule of his injections, the Dietrich Nurse's routine—how everyone in the hospital is attractive and how this attractiveness makes Pike unconscionably nervous.

The boy of sixteen gestates *U* and *O* sounds—as if overripe with lumbago, punished by the divine monad distributing pain to sinners—he looks like a sinner. Pike's mind drifts back to the operating table—General David Petraeus jumping out of an airplane in 1999, his chute malfunctioning and dropping to the ground hard—cracking his pelvis—the boy of sixteen's pregnant vowels—"It was scary at the time," Sixtus Petraeus says, "but you don't know my David"—and by all accounts, David Petraeus is *a real go-getter*—Leibniz's best of all possible worlds and at its center David Petraeus—and the White Fingered Doctor exhaling slowly, and the Secondary Doctor, vowing to vote for Petraeus should he ever run for public office—and the Bradley Nurse—he knows that she was there—but Pike has no memory of the Bradley Nurse—even though he can recognize her when he sees her, and he has seen her many times—but like Indianapolis's sister city, Springfield, Illinois, a ghost of a big-box facade—and though composed of flesh and blood—immediate, human, and tactile—the Bradley Nurse is almost entirely imaginary—she does not have the face for it.

Pike decides that he cannot wait until tomorrow—the risk is too high—and between then and now he is far too vulnerable—not risking mere suffocation, but something as yet unseen—something sinister—and the boy next to Pike passively and politely offers up his name, wheezing—and his name is disregarded—Pike does not care about his name, but war, self-preservation, the spring in the Dietrich Nurse's step—and with some trouble he detaches the tubes leading to his blood stream—the envelope of his body compromised—and he gathers up his belongings—his white wool pants, his brown leather shoes, the interview with Sixtus Petraeus—and Pike exits the room and enters the yellow hallway on his own two feet.

"I am not terrified," he reminds himself—two men ignoring Pike to his immediate right—two steps more and still nothing, no eyes, no doctors, no orderlies with sedatives—as it had often been with Pike's successes—marked by a deep-set confusion, fear, the workings of accident—and judging by the two men's faces, Pike must be a visitor or a pharmaceutical rep—but not a patient, not a prisoner, not running down a hallway of intermittent black—a rainbow möbius strip leading to nowhere—and yet, the real patients also seem to come and go as they please, the ones obviously patients—from their rooms freely, walking the hallway and stretching their legs—to the bath and back, the courtyard, the hospital loggia—and an elderly woman wheeling her IV smiles at Pike—and the Secondary Doctor waves at him from down the hall—smiling—the same hand that had undoubtedly entered his stomach—a sick kind of normal—where was the organizing principle, where was Le Corbusier, a way to make sense of it all—no big brother to blame, but everyone, anyone, Pike surely included, horribly and irrevocably responsible—and at that point it's far too diluted—and Pike pushes past the two men and rushes for the door, down the stairs and through the lobby—the outside air of Indianapolis.

Pike breathes again like during the operation, pulling oxygen into his lungs quickly—inhale and out—bill and coo—the clean air a cheap seduction—and not because of its purity, its exhaust, its flecks of dust—by that measure it is as dirty as any—but it feels clean to Pike in a way different than the hospital antiseptic—as if those beautiful sick particles were rubbed smooth with fine rags—Johnny Walker Blue and not Johnny Walker Black—and Pike feels intoxicated just breathing outside—the skateboarding pregnant woman wearing a helmet only for herself—the man on the sidewalk, a pacifist bonobo—and their respective indiscriminant declarations of war—Pike runs two blocks to put a space between himself and the hospital—sucking in air a different kind of dirty—humid and grainy, not hermetically sealed—and at the intersection, two more benign white men—the man reading *USA Today* peaceably vomiting.

The sun strikes Pike's skin and burns at each flexed layer of cells—sweat and sebaceous glands below the epidermis—flayed and peeled like fresh incisions—and the two-toned sky accept-

ing Pike in spite of all his faults—tracing his
movements and throwing down sulfur—the sun's
fixed tracks across the sky. It couldn't be this easy,
Pike thinks—to escape onto a sidewalk so man-
icured and symmetrical—too symmetrical perhaps—attractive faces mirrored perfectly down
the center line marring the torqued distortions
of real beauty—Pike eases his stride and turns
to look behind him—the grass meeting the concrete edge—the imposing War Memorial and
the high rises beyond—enclosing him within
like foothills—fences or wooden stakes in the
ground—the force of wind shear on skyscrapers—
to bend and snap in sudden cataclysmic failure.

In his personal theodicy Pike assumes a certain
amount of free will—finding a bench and reading
the Sixtus Petraeus interview more closely—he
notices something curious amongst the questions
about Sixtus's immigration from Holland—the fact
that he is a sea captain—questions about David as a
boy and as a young man—almost in passing, Sixtus
Petraeus offers up that he is a fan of the Japanese
boy band S.M.A.P—their 2008 release, the album
Super Modern Artistic Performance—and J-pop more
broadly—it's all fantastic—their matching tailored
suits and thin-thin waists measured in centime-
ters—their frankness in their own plasticity—it is

the last song to make Sixtus Petraeus cry, he says—
S.M.A.P's "Sad Song"—and of course, what other
song to make you cry but "Sad Song," Pike thinks—
though he wonders why this portion of the interview
was not edited out, whether *The New York Times* is
also going the way of the tabloid, perfect bald Dem-
ocrats in turtlenecks, and what was meant by its in-
clusion, which he knows is the wrong question to ask.

The bench on the square is made of concrete formed
into the shape of a plush couch—there is the impression of softness—Pike engulfed by a thick envelope of down and the liquid stone hardened so
that he can feel its tension lines—sensing that he
will be safe here—in his street clothes still a pharmaceutical rep—and this seems like something
a pharmaceutical rep would do, Pike thinks—to
sit on a concrete couch at midday, not attracting
undo attention. There are men and women passing and he looks for those in isolation to ask them
what day it is—shouting out a little too abruptly
"What day is it?"—and "Tuesday" the woman with
the mouth answers—but it couldn't be a Tuesday,
he went into the hospital on a Tuesday—and had
it been one week or two, or was it the very same
day—time now blocked and not strung on a line—
and Pike cries out to the woman "But what week
then"—though the woman refuses to respond, or

not knowing how—weeks not measured like days and months with a name—no longer a pharmaceutical rep but a panhandler or war veteran gone crazy—and he must move from the bench, Pike thinks, more fitting to sit on the sidewalk space—David Petraeus slapping the steel frame of the airplane with a grin, parachuting in full commando gear.

He tries to collect himself—think—who can be trusted—the White Fingered Doctor, no; the Bradley Nurse, no; the woman with the mouth—certainly not—and from the stone couch Pike looks out onto the War Memorial at the center of Indianapolis—an inherently French space with the echoes of the École—Pike doesn't trust that either—not the work of a Ledoux or Lebrouste, but some cheap American imitation incapable of even doing French right. At one corner of the memorial, a couple in their sixties sit with their shopping bags—at the other end a blond Alsatian man of mixed stock looks directly at Pike—and what is he looking at—his white pants, his *New York Times*—the Alsatian staring—and when Pike breaks eye contact, the Alsatian continues to stare—a buzz on Pike's face—a cloud—he feels himself being dissected, feels in his periphery the set of eyes upon him—and the Alsatian must be filthy, Pike thinks in self-defense, a sweating mass unaccustomed to the humidity—and rising to his full height, the Alsatian eyes Pike with even more concentration.

Pike turns and walks away from the plaza—ten meters, twenty—slowly now, and turning his head behind him—no, he cannot spot the Alsatian over his shoulder—no longer at the corner of the War Memorial, but Pike does not dare to stop—he has the distinct feeling that he is being followed—being watched—during the operation, recalling the silver tray of knives and instruments beside the operating table—knowing that these tools would be used against him—and now with the windows overlooking the sidewalk and strangers on the street all watching—the image of the man begins to shift in his mind—his face appearing on another with dark hair—his canary-yellow shoes on the feet of a woman—Pike accelerates and turns down a side street—and like the Bradley Nurse, Pike worries that he will not be able to recognize the man should he see him again.

He slips off the road and into a pub—its walls covered in curio ornaments—rubber and ivory and sepia photographs of big-game safaris—Pike positions himself with his eyes on the door—not to be conspicuous—and introduces himself to a man who says his name is Eysenck and the man beside him from Nordrhein Westfalen, who speaks as if he is from Wisconsin and not Westphalia—Eysenck expressing his firm belief in primogeniture—"Otherwise all your lands will divided," he explains. Pike agrees with a nod—he watches the door—Eysenck explaining the concept of comparative intelligence—how the conception of genius, as being somehow superhuman, is a common misconception—not elevated or divine, but flattened and essential—more flawed, more leveled, more practiced and vulnerable—Pike nods again, and the bar hums with the drone of a beetle—elytra and pinchers and snow from the television—and Pike contributes to the conversation somewhat hesitantly with brief comments on *vectors of fear* and *Sixtus Petraeus.*

The man Eysenck extends the back of his hand to his forehead as if resigned to some great ecstasy or disgust—with little in between—with little endearing ulcers one simply wants to cater to—"A recovered or recovering alcoholic," Eysenck says—breathing with his whole body—not a wheeze, not like the boy of sixteen, but with the diaphragm of a Shylock or a woodwose prepared to scream. Pike ignores him and keeps his eyes on the door. The last three people to have entered look just like the Alsatian, but they do not look at all like one another: the man in the black vest, the attractive woman like Marlene Dietrich, the naval cadet in his uniform. Pike imagines the cadet shoveling coal into a boiler to punish him—feeding the flame with a great bellows—how he is from New Jersey, how his name is Johnny, how he competes for the attention of a Helen with another man named Joe—and breaking into Pike's daydream, Eysenck reaches out and grabs the cadet with both hands and draws him in close to whispering distance.

"Do you know my friend Mr. Pike" Eysenck says, "you make him nervous. You make it so he keeps looking at you and can't listen to my story"—and all human societies are either *guilt cultures* or *shame cultures*, Pike thinks—in the case of shame translating through familial, state, and cultural lines—in the case of guilt centered on one's own actions. "Do you want to hear my story," Eysenck continues, not waiting for an answer—holding the cadet close to his cigarette face—breathing with his whole body—Pike feeling both shame and guilt simultaneously, and he wonders whether the cadet is the Alsatian or no—reciting a small prayer:

> *Nothing can be causa sui a cause unto itself.*
> *In order to be morally responsible, one must*
> *be causa sui, a cause unto itself.*
> *No one can be truly morally responsible for*
> *their actions.*

Eysenck makes eye contact with his associ-
ate from Westphalia—revenge for what exactly,
Pike thinks—and what will they do with him—
Eysenck losing interest—and just as quickly as he had sought to destroy him, he abruptly
lets the cadet go—running to meet his party at
a far table—and Eysenck returns unconsciously to his drink and his explication of genius.

The cadet Johnny, Pike realizes, is not the Alsatian—not a spy, not following him—but one of a
dozen cadets in the pub, though temporally confusing, celebrating self-assuredly like it's May 8,
1945—and of course your war is just when you're
fighting Nazis, Pike thinks—at least on film—
the macro scale of nation-state and net measured
atrocities—Bentham's moral calculus. The cadets
are all clean shaven—they move en masse and
shuttle between their table and the bar—faceless
in their uniforms—and it is confusing to Pike
why there is suddenly a U.S. naval presence in
Indianapolis with no significant bodies of water
nearby—and confusing that if it is not Johnny,
the Alsatian must still be out there somewhere.

The two other possibilities, the man with the black
vest and the attractive woman like Marlene Dietrich, are talking at a nearby table—the man's

hair is the color of champagne, a flirt—and the woman divides her attention between the man in the black vest and her glances up and around the bar—as if she is looking for something, looking for Pike perhaps—and they lean in close and talk closer—the single Alsatian divided now into two bodies—one and the same—joining together again—the intersection of parallel lines in curved space—dangerous, Pike thinks—incestuous, asexual—the marrying-off of first cousins to preserve familial lines—and while Eysenck perhaps might approve, Pike certainly cannot.

He keeps his eyes on the pair of Alsatians—sharing a kiss, the man's hand resting on the woman's back—they drink and talk closer—talking about what exactly—precision of knowledge, precision of hand, control always evading Pike—and their words just beyond his hearing—*bomb* the man's lips seem to say, or is it *bulb*, that roundest of words enveloping Pike like Aris Kindt's *alluvial*—or *Tom*, Thomas, the Alsatian's name perhaps—finally something Pike can use—and the attractive woman like Marlene Dietrich signs to pay their check—they stand and stand close to one another—and like a whisper—*the White Fingered Doctor*, their lips seem to say—Pike's attention flaring red—the White Fingered Doctor—what connection—listening more closely to what is still out of reach—the Alsatians walking farther away from Pike, arm and arm—stopping for a full two minutes at the back of the pub at the bath—as if time has suspended—and then stepping outside and leaving together.

At the other end of the bar Pike sees the naval cadets converging on Eysenck and the man from Westphalia—a groundswell of hate surfacing in their greatest of generations' innocence. Johnny and the largest of the cadets, clearly their primal leader in situations of ancestral hunt—at the points when democracy is abandoned and chiefs are chosen on the basis of killing capacity alone—points at Eysenck's chest in questioning—points at Pike across the bar—and they stare at him like the Alsatian stared—ushering Pike into the huddle—wanting desperately to follow the Alsatian couple outside, but forced back in to the throng—wanting to say something conciliatory and meek, or profane and loud, but managing neither and simply whimpering—"Hold on," Eysenck says—his speech is one of surprising inebriated calm—and the naval cadets are poised to kill—an accelerating system—with each nominal incremental gain in hate, feeding throughout an exponential output—"In this situation," Eysenck asks, "what would General Petraeus do?"—and while by no means winning the argument, the cadets are at least somewhat stunned, their moral compass called into question.

The huge cadet's face morphs into an expression of uncertainty and stoicism—looking at Eysenck as if not knowing how to manage—or knowing exactly how but deciding whether to act or no—and Pike needs to get outside—needs to know how the White Fingered Doctor is involved—what did they want with him; why were they following him—though seeing no positive move to make Pike has no choice except but to fail to act—waiting passively for another's decision—Eysenck with at least the capacity to speak, to argue—and the huge cadet seemingly more confused than convinced in the justice of retribution—and yet at the same time unwilling to withdraw—unwilling to make peace and unwilling to declare outright war—the huge cadet seems to compromise by somewhat halfheartedly laying several quick blows to Pike, Eysenck, and the man from Westphalia— not to the face, and not out to maim—but just enough for the receiver to go fetal and bask in it.

The cadets return to their table somewhat disappointed, still bottled up and poised—and Eysenck—after having spent a moment to himself on the linoleum, and after having slowly regained his feet—really truly very pleased with the outcome, buys a round for the three of them in celebration— the man from Westphalia is pleased too, holding his stomach—and Pike, worried that he may be losing the Alsatians forever, and not really knowing what to do besides drink, takes the gin and pineapple juice that is offered to him and swallows—feeling in spite of himself a fleeting closeness to and sympathy for these men—the kind only mutual suffering elicits—an apologetic and conditional nostalgia—wishing that the suffering had never occurred, but since it had, and if it was written on high, Pike was glad to have suffered with these men.

He excuses himself and exits the pub, early afternoon and still bright, and Pike wonders if it is still Tuesday or whether time is once again slipping—if the medication in his system is making him more sensitive to sunlight—more prone to tendon failure or rupture of any kind—he glances in both directions down the street, looking for the Alsatian couple but seeing only a man with his spaniel—the punctuated holes in the asphalt and anonymous windows, as big as a butterfly—he chooses west, acting on instinct, and shuffles in that direction— as smoke begins to rise from the pub behind him— his leather shoes toeing and heeling the street surface—the asphalt shifts into wet cinder pavers.

Pike recalls two books that he has recently read and admired, both by the same author, a contemporary New York poet—who, Pike has heard, in his sure-of-himself sensibility, suffers from an unnatural swelling of the neck and eyes—the first, a novel, is all about soil: its constitutive parts of sand and clay—dark loam, silt, and sweet bio-matter—aeration, worms, humus—digesting microbes—the whole system a grand exposed stomach breathing death—though Pike did not find the novel nihilistic as some reviewers criticized, but really on point with the state of the matter—not "A failed and blind satire of nothingness," as one critic pointedly described it, but, and like his later works, willing in Pike's opinion to question the current state of patience and good taste.

In the second, also a novel, two rival boiler room operators fall in love with the same woman, Helen, their superior officer and commander aboard the U.S.S. *Areola*, who has feelings for them both, and while choosing between her Joe and her Johnny, Helen must weigh the state of her command and the war effort more broadly against her erotic impulses to act—though throughout the great majority of the work, it is simply the two operators shoveling coal into the ship's boilers—a good

220 pages of shoveling—and continuing along his
westerly path, Pike realizes that he is back at the
War Memorial—and how had he come here—certain that at all times he had this point in space at
his back—and two blocks ahead Pike can see the
hospital's rectangular silhouette—inconspicuously
hideous, its rectangular windows, its rectangular
doors—and the adjacent parking structure held
fast on all sides—with no room to breathe—cycling heat and cold, expansion and contraction—
full of cracks and literally tearing itself apart.

Pike stands at the base of the memorial where the
Alsatian once stood, looking at the sidewalk as if he
can see the imprint of his shoes, the echo or vestige
of the man in the space he once occupied—like the
dead, Pike thinks, the Alsatian—a ghost or a daemon—refusing to fade but attaching himself to anyone and everyone, the void in the air, haunting and
building up like sediment—Pike walks clear around
the memorial to get a sense of its scale—the way he
can feel it even with his eyes closed through the
sublte shifts in reverberation—the shallow silence
of rock, the deep chatter and swallow of the plaza—
and he sits down on the couch where the elderly couple's shopping bags once rested—a deep anxiety—
and Pike is once again afraid—the sun still shining
at midday—too bright and hot to his skin and eyes.

In the hospital, the Bradley Nurse had tested Pike's lung capacity by having Pike blow into a tube—the tube connected to a graduated cylinder marked with unitless measures, and inside a small plastic bead that rises with the intake of air sticks at its highest point to provide a reading—though what that had to do with his own vestigial removal Pike was uncertain, or what the face of the Bradley Nurse really looked like—his medication may or may not be affecting his memory, may or may not be increasing his sensitivity to sunlight—and for those with a history of epilepsy, PTSD, central nervous system problems broadly, Pike's medication should "Under no circumstances be taken at all," the Bradley Nurse had said—the calm in her tone, the matter-of-fact nature of it all—and perhaps he did have a history but that that history was unknown to him, or a disease lying dormant waiting for its time and place to react, the unique set of circumstances that will bring it to the fore.

Pike looks out at the hospital and the human figures and frames moving in and out of its doors—perhaps one of them is the White Fingered Doctor, or the pair of Alsatians, the Bradley Nurse with her unconscious and unnatural sense of calm—all conspiring together, making some small but assertive declaration of war, Pike thinks—fully desensitized to the human cost, and weighing the odd abstraction higher than Pike's or any other patient's most basic and fundamental welfare—they're frauds, Pike thinks—posing as doctors—smoking cigarettes and laughing—the faceless Bradley Nurse, in a steam room in Winston-Salem with only the most attractive of Philip Morris representatives—and if there was nothing wrong with Pike to start with, what had they really done to him on the operating table—why had the Alsatians doubled and multiplied, following his every move—and why when he was so sure that he was traveling away from the War Memorial did he come back attracted like a magnet. Pike can hear his heart monitor racing in the fashion of a phantom limb—listening intently to the no-longer attached, the no-longer beeping.

He moves closer to the hospital to get a better look at its entrance—two men in white scrubs with shower-cap booties over their shoes stand to its north side and breathe with percussive exhales, biting their bottom lips and gnashing their teeth in a kind of hyena pleasure—their booties preventing the blood and human filth from staining their shoes—the speakers outside of the hospital blaring the title track of S.M.A.P.'s *Super Modern*

Artistic Performance. It makes the two men move their shoulders in smooth revolutions, a dance and gyration disconnected in Pike's opinion from the care of their fellow man—moving like periscopes vertically on axes and rotating and fluttering like modern jazz. Adjacent to the two men, the hospital's front door opens and closes automatically— at times opening for no one at all—or for a man with a cowboy hat exiting with a certain self-assurance wearing plaid—whose name is unlikely to be Driggers, though Pike thinks it should be.

The cowboy lights a cigarette with a raw health and vitality that convinces Pike in that instant that there is no connection between cancer and smoking—he wears Wranglers and a belt buckle in the pattern of a giant chrome Star of David—and Pike decides to wait—watches Driggers smoke slowly— as if breathing is not a necessity for Driggers but Eden's sweet honey—the air capacity of a sperm whale—how Driggers can hold his breath for a good ninety minutes and ride even the most destructive of bulls for a full eight seconds—and Pike is uncertain of how long he waits there—hours or minutes, the sun still high at midday—and the entrance doors continue to open and close, breaking in timed intervals the hospital's tight hermetic seal.

In the New York poet's novel about soil, Pike recalls a particular extended section on *trees*—the way trees act in isolation and the way groups or communities of trees act collectively to form *forests*, in some cases *rain forests* which are critical to world oxygen supplies—and while criticized for lacking a certain humanity—the stark grayscale of black and white—Pike finds the novel's section on trees particularly moving—in its way—the manner in which the item is essentialized, the belief in the pure realization of an idea unclouded by nuance or fact— the paradigmatic unicorn running through a field of wheat—Hume's idealized stallion no longer an impossible conception but real—or real enough— and that purity seems important to Pike—for the alignment of language if for nothing else—seeing in Driggers not aspects of a cowboy, but the paradigm realized, smoking outside of the hospital.

In Indianapolis, bold Speer-like Art Deco towers rise from the ground's surface and cast great shadows over the downtown War Memorial, the city hospital, the Broad Ripple district full of hippies, and with the sun directly overhead Pike sees her, not expecting or knowing what he's been waiting for exactly until now, before he does—and coloring and rewriting his past to say that he's been waiting for the Dietrich Nurse the whole time—

waiting for something, and she happened to be it—like falling in love Pike thinks—always from without and beyond the will—the Dietrich Nurse steps swiftly down the lobby stairs. The sensor on the door opens the glass before her, and the Dietrich Nurse strides past the two dancing men in white and past the cowboy Driggers deliberately.

Pike tails the Dietrich Nurse south along the avenue, her white surface casting a blue shadow on the sidewalk—her canary-yellow shoes and the backs of her legs when she walks appear differently on the street than from Pike's view on the gurney—not with a shot to deliver or mechanically utilitarian, but artful and voluntary—the space between her ankles and knees creates dark shifting candlesticks—the negative space outside of the circle—to be burned, Pike thinks—to be followed—and the Dietrich Nurse paws the ground gingerly with the balls of her feet—Pike several meters back—and between them a mother and child, both barely capable of walking—Pike is amazed that they don't simply topple and that humans can stand upright at all—and compared to the Dietrich Nurse, the mother is all red and gangly.

The Dietrich Nurse enters a drug store—the television above the checkout playing over the customers—"Johnny has his own daemons, don't you Johnny?" the television says—and the Dietrich Nurse fills a prescription at the counter and picks something off of a shelf that Pike cannot see, while Johnny on the television refuses to answer. She must know something, Pike thinks—what is she taking off of the shelf—why would she fill her prescription here and not at the hospital—and Pike knows that the White Fingered Doctor is not to be trusted, but perhaps the Dietrich Nurse can be—though she certainly played her part when they strapped him down—her uncanny resemblance to the woman at the pub—the way that they're following him—and Pike looks in through the display window from outside of the drug store—its expressionless mannequins in the mold of the Dietrich Nurse—displaying women's Wranglers.

The Dietrich Nurse exits and continues along on foot—and she must live close by, Pike thinks—he follows her to the grocery where she buys staples and to a four-story walk-up in the shape of a great rectangle with windows to the street as clear as the drug store's display. Pike can see the lights flick on when she enters her apartment—home alone, he thinks—and he feels her silhouette as it passes in front of the window—her mere presence having the effect on him so as to contemplate that presence—a desire to increase his intake of air—and while others are coldly dropped from consciousness as soon as they enter his mind—the only way to sort out all of the data, Pike thinks—the Dietrich Nurse lingers and hides there—the mannequin is always selling—and not what it's wearing—even when bald and naked selling the idea of what could or should be.

Outside of the Dietrich Nurse's apartment, he watches the variable shadow behind the curtain—lightening and darkening—sometimes reflecting clearly the imprint of the Dietrich Nurse herself, but then there are other shapes and forms more jagged and industrial, or smooth and organic, tiny arrangements of trees and naval ships, or a coin being flipped—up and rotating back—the shadow is cast twice, and each time it slips further from its referent and deeper into Pike's viewing so that he knows that the Dietrich Nurse is not home alone, but that someone is up there with her—a lover or a villain, someone sinister and red—with gangly arms and a jagged face—and the villain places his giant palm on the Dietrich Nurse's forehead—and for an instant the silhouette of the villain reveals himself—the silhouette of Le Modular—his arm raised and poised to strike—the light switches off and the window blackens.

Pike knows it is wrong to run but he does so anyway—across the opposite sidewalk to the handle
of the four-story's entrance—shaking hands with
the building, he knows at once that the Dietrich
Nurse is in danger and threatened—threatened by
a phantom or daemon that he will not be able to
see in the flesh—not dependent on any external
real, but upon his actions, his will, his thoughts
and ideas—caught and trapped—and if he fails
to act the villain will surely have his way with
her—the Dietrich Nurse punished—and if he
does, the villain will simply cease to exist—fade
from view back to shadow with a smirk, as if to
say yes, you've won, but you've made yourself out
to be mad in the process—and she will never believe that the villain's hand was about to strike—
never believe what Pike knows to be true—and
how he'll be relegated to the sidewalk space as
a casualty of war—the Dietrich Nurse stepping
past him ungratefully, stepping past deliberately.

Pike opens the door to the stairwell, while above the
Modular Man stands behind the Dietrich Nurse
with his palm raised—the Modular Man divided
by the golden section—the ratio between the extension of his reach to his height—his middle to the
whole—more perfect than Pike and more pleasing

to the eye—a villain completely predictable though increasingly dangerous—threatening the Dietrich Nurse who is fully unaware—if something should happen, Pike would be responsible because he allowed it to happen—it is worse than striking the blow himself, because at least in that case he claims responsibility—and Pike spans the first stretch of risers taking two steps at a time—spinning around the corner of the banister and using his arm like a spoke on a wheel—and he sees the street-facing apartments in front of him, the internal brick—and he sees the Dietrich Nurse herself, calmly walking down the steps—not trailed by a daemon but rattling her keys—and Pike freezes on the stair that he is standing on, breathing hard, laboring—meeting the eyes of the Dietrich Nurse—and "Mr. Pike?" she says, "what are you doing here?"

Perhaps the White Fingered Doctor had sent Le Modular—the villain just beyond the door—patient and waiting for the Dietrich Nurse to return—to destroy Pike now, or at least his credibility, and the Dietrich Nurse later—or perhaps the Modular Man is one and the same as the Alsatian—his shifting face, shifting shadow—or that he has already acted, Pike thinks—the Dietrich Nurse's prescription filled, a poison or placebo, not actively assertive but removing what's palliative—

how the Dietrich Nurse is also inflicted by a disease
lying dormant, an unknown history. Pike can feel
his tongue crumble before its own weight—a slight
lightheadedness, a floating feeling—unable to explain his presence on the landing, or the danger in
which they find themselves—no lie or truth could
possibly explain—and why were they following
him, Pike thinks—reminding himself of the fact
that he is not terrified, not mad—hearing the rat-
tle of the Dietrich Nurse's keys on the stairs above.

Pike does not answer and nor does he move for
what seems like a long time—part and partial of
self-sacrifice, Pike thinks—someone's if not his
own—and the grout between the bricks oozes between its horizontal courses as if frozen in continual tension—the Dietrich Nurse refusing to
move either—and Pike, not knowing what to do
besides run, rotates quickly on axis and steps toward the exit—"Excuse me" he says, trying not to
make any abrupt movements as he turns for the
stairs—imagining that he has an umbrella in his
hand to steady himself on a tightrope—imagining himself breaking in on the Modular Man and
the Dietrich Nurse just at the moment before
the Modular Man is about to strike, throwing a
shoe at him or whatever is handy, and the ensuing
tussle—though Pike is stronger—and he lowers

and folds the great Modular Man to his knees—
breaking the proportion of his golden section.

*

Pike tries not to look backwards and takes several
quick turns on side streets to break his path from
that of the Dietrich Nurse. It seems only polite,
Pike thinks—and his eyes move to the sidewalk
to look for any conch shell or lotus flower baring the mark of Le Modular, the proportions of
the golden section—distrustful at best of those
on the street who are too symmetrical or too attractive—and surely there must be something
wrong with them—something morally and eth-
ically dubious—how those who are particularly
handsome are conspiring against him—entitled
by their own beauty—and in the built landscape,
Pike feels precisely the inverse—how buildings
which are principled and proportional are virtuous and trustworthy—and how the City Hospital houses all kinds of profane and impious
acts—its canary-yellow halls—its rational logics.

It was Pike's intention to lose the Dietrich Nurse,
to shake himself free of her on the city streets
where he has been drawn in and trapped—framed
and made out to be mad so that the Dietrich Nurse

could not listen or respond honestly to a version of himself who is sane, rather than one who is crazy—through forces outside of his control and for reasons well beyond mere volition—Pike is drawn back by exactly what he is trying to escape. As he turns past the office park, Pike can see the Dietrich Nurse talking to a pale-skinned thin man in a dark jacket—a vampire, Pike thinks—intention and politeness be damned—the Dietrich Nurse undoubtedly having left her apartment shortly after him—so that Pike has unwittingly, and completely beyond his will, silently circled around again behind her.

The man's face is perfectly symmetrical and pale but not without pigment—too attractive to be trusted and too round and clean and straightforward to actually exist in the form he presents himself—he must be masked or much dirtier, Pike thinks—and from his own understanding of the man, this seems consistent—an obvious facade and the outside layer of many—Pike desiring the whole truth no matter how disruptive or impossible—one clean statement that can be taken as complete in and of itself—and while he is unable to hear their conversation, Pike can see their lips moving—he inches in closer and listens to the sounds outside and those unrelated—determined to find out what is going on.

It is as if he is watching a pair of mimes—the vampire in black and the Dietrich Nurse wrapped in her white uniform—outside of earshot and moving their arms—the man tells the Dietrich Nurse that there is a disease spreading, Pike thinks—making advances upon her or arranging a meeting with the White Fingered Doctor—they stand flatfooted facing one another shoulder to shoulder—they plant their feet square and still upon the ground—and he must be a vampire or some other kind of villain to stand so unnaturally, Pike thinks—rigid like a marine or a drum major—Pike feels like he too is being watched—he scans the windows on the north side of the street and then the south—those covered in loose curtains or filled with air conditioning units—a sickness in the air that must be filtered and cooled—and Pike knows they are looking down upon him.

While it is against his nature to wish violence or ill will upon the vampire, and admitting to himself that despite his suspicions he in fact knows almost nothing about him, Pike feels a desire, slight and perhaps not real, but pointed and tangible, to take the man by the shoulders and throw him violently to the sidewalk—to lock him up to marinate for ninety days in Zionsville, Indiana—below grade in some nice home in the sub-urbs—and afterwards make him talk—to con-fess to crimes as yet uncommitted—and Pike considers interrupting them then and there, to rush between them and tear them apart, perhaps without talking at all himself or asking any ques-tions—questions having gotten Pike nowhere—but to defraud, cuckold, beat the vampire soundly.

Pike recalls the list of adjectives on the back cov-er of the New York poet's novel: *huge, inflamma-tory, powerful, brilliant*—he imagines applying this list to himself and feels more confident—the man in black and the Dietrich Nurse now walk in opposite directions—the vampire pass-ing Pike—unaware of his presence. Pike falls in drop step behind the man in black, emboldened by necessity or hubris to follow closer than he had with the Dietrich Nurse, wanting to hear what the vampire might be saying—to listen to his breath, his wheeze, his exhale—to get up close to his skin like a great Brobdingnagian breast and look at his pores and feel sickened—to see the city expand in its inescapable and diluted beige.

Pike turns when the man turns—matches him step for step—mirroring his body position down the avenue where the Dietrich Nurse lives and three blocks further—several quick turns and the street opens back up onto the plaza of the War Memorial. A panic consumes Pike as if he were back at the gallows, and the man turns around at the same moment with a puzzled and irritated look—"Can I help you?"—encroaching on Pike's space, pushing him backwards, swelling up like a peacock—and just as quickly promptly vanishing—leaving Pike to stare up at the War Memorial's stone mass.

In truth, Pike considers himself a coward when it comes to physical violence and finds this position logically consistent with his other beliefs—prioritized self-preservation, determinism, and free will—as if it were the 1980's and a good time for chauvinism—when he could be much braver and work himself into top physical condition—and not for purely cosmetic reasons either, but the threat of mutual destruction should things ever come to a fight—with no real intention of ever using his newly formed strength—but for putting on airs—and the vampires of the world may be more vindictive perhaps, but compared to Pike they are just as false and just as swelling.

Pike abandons cardinal directions and hikes away from the War Memorial at a diagonal. With little concern for where he is going, he narrows his field of vision forward like lowering blinders on a horse—and sticking to the path that he has plotted for himself—against the grain of the buildings, the grid, the street fronts—he crosses block upon block and cuts through lawns and the thousands of acres of grass written into the building code. Pike jogs around homes and office buildings when necessary, but returns quickly to his diagonal, a saw tooth line bisecting the city, and it does not take long to leave downtown and enter a residential neighborhood with which Pike is unfamiliar—with small square fenced-in yards that he climbs over—dropping into a chain-linked pen with an RV in the drive and a rusted metal swing-set on the lawn certainly outgrown by those for whom it was built.

In the hospital they had placed a syringe into Pike's stomach, and he could see the needle enter his body a good four inches—surprised that it did not go straight through him and hit the metal plane of the surgical table below—just a tiny prick and suddenly diving clear through his soft tissue, his internal organs, his skin on the other side of his body—and cowardice, while socially frowned upon, certainly seems a genetic advantage, in tuned to logic, Pike thinks—and he takes note of a large boilermaker approaching from the sliding glass door on the home. While those with RVs are on a very fundamental level much scarier than those without RVs—having something to do with their relative preparedness when it comes to survival situations—the boilermaker asks him if he needs any help, a phone, something cold to drink—expressing a kindly and confused Hoosier hospitality to Pike, who stands blankly and uninvited in the backyard—failing to engage or seemingly to recognize the boilermaker's questions at all.

The boilermaker is attractive with a symmetrical face, and this seems ominous. What does it take, Pike thinks, to find some ordinary, trustworthy, unattractive people, to be bored or to kill time in meaningless pursuits, or to over-eat and feel sluggish and fail to move because you're incapable of moving—though it is novel, Pike concedes, to receive some measure of charity—and it would be a great coincidence indeed if the boilermaker is involved with the White Fingered Doctor—impossible even—the odds being too great to calculate—and considering his risk, "Yes," Pike says, "I'd love something to drink," admittedly thirsty from his walk through the city. The boilermaker, somewhat taken aback, retreats into the house to fetch a pitcher, and of the two kinds of charity, his is not the variety distributed by evangelists who like to loudly pontificate on their evangelizing, but the much more distant, much safer kind given by those who do not expect to be taken up on their offers.

The boilermaker returning from the house pours Pike a tall glass of ice water and offers him a seat on the lawn furniture—hard plastic woven through a metal frame like a basket—and taking the adjacent seat himself, the boilermaker asks Pike his name and if he is lost and if he needs a taxi—to be pitied—and Pike, believing that the true humanitarian act cannot have pity at its core, grows resentful because the boilermaker believes he to be mad—and instead of taking the offered taxi, Pike decides to remain silent and to stare at the boilermaker for four minutes exactly—four full minutes, Pike tells himself—and he looks up at the boilermaker, while taking in generous swallows from his glass, refilling it from the pitcher, and drinking more slowly, his eyes fixed on the boilermaker, and perhaps he is not to be trusted after all.

Pike counts in his head from *one* to *thirty* slowly and then down again, repeating when he gets back to zero, and raising his index finger to the boilermaker to indicate *one*—to indicate *two*—the boilermaker sitting in his lawn chair, patient for the first minute becomes increasingly agitated as Pike begins raising his fingers in sequence without explanation—asking why Pike is staring, why he is methodically raising his digits, why won't he speak when he was speaking before—Pike indicating *three*—and the boilermaker leaves his seat and steps backwards toward the sliding glass door—Pike raises his gaze and continues to silently stare—taking a long sip from his glass, the ice bumping against his upper lip, the condensation building up around the glass, and the tiny particles of water wiped clear by Pike's grip—the mark of his fingertips—the reverberating ice echoes in sharp harmonic tinks and deadened clucks as the boilermaker inches away—the scuff of his shoes—Pike indicating *four* with his pinky—and "Thank you for the drink," Pike says—standing up slowly—and he exits through the fence's latched gate.

For all his kindness and charity, Pike prefers the cowboy Driggers to the boilermaker and his lot—preferring abstraction and character type and paradigm to the subtlety of real human beings—and if he treated everyone as a real human being, Pike believes he would be completely paralyzed—incapable of having a conversation with a boilermaker—but a cowboy, he knows how to appreciate, to approach—a way of sifting the data—a generic sleight of hand—where the cowboy Driggers perhaps is in fact a real human being—perhaps he is not—but to function, Pike must believe him to be a cowboy and a cowboy he is to Pike—while the boilermakers of the world waffle and gripe and act erratically, individually demanding individualized attention, and providing their pity-filled charity that Pike simply will not stand for.

The boilermaker behind him, Pike feels somewhat adrift—floating through neighborhoods created from a single house plan—one master clone and hundreds of copies in neat organized rows—all painted beige and with greenish lawns and American flags—where American nationalism is most alive—the suburbs and neighborhoods most detached and most easily reproducible—with Pike on foot and the sun fully overhead at midday—filtered and softened through concentric layers of white—a high-pressure system of overcast clouds—the buses of freshly dry-cleaned naval cadets in cattle cars passing him on the sidewalk—a line of six blue 1992 Ford Tauruses all in a row—and there is something curious about Indianapolis, Pike thinks—something or someone pushing him in directions only partially his choosing.

A low clicking sound snaps Pike to consciousness—a reawakening of the body and of the velocity of his mass through space and time—the clicks coming from behind and increasing in volume and intensity, a pushing sense of urgency like the bottled stress of someone entering a room, a pressure seeping from one body to the next—and turning, Pike can see two businessmen following him with briefcases and umbrellas and hats to match their suits. They walk next to one another with the air of the city, out of context from the gabled roofs and lawns of the suburban street—their awful above-ground pools like giant snare drums, American flags and ceramic water fowl, houses too big for the lots—and as Pike turns at the next block, the businessmen turn with him, not looking or staring, but turning when he turns, gaining on Pike and closing the gap between them.

Pike increases his pace but does not want to cause a scene or to call undo attention to himself—does not want to turn around so as to have the businessmen see him looking—but even with his eyes faced front Pike can feel their presence—he can hear the clicking of their wingtips and his own breath increase its cadence—Pike in the lead and the businessmen trailing like ducklings behind him. He takes another turn down a street that appears identical to the last, hoping that the businessmen will go straight and fail to follow—that perhaps he is paranoid or overeager—seeing in ink blots: the

White Fingered Doctor, the industrial accident, a body that is either dead or dying—one false interpretation among many—and how navigating the city is less about being right, but knowing truth to be impossible and limiting oneself to being slightly less wrong than one otherwise might be—and yet the businessmen do turn—they do follow—multiplied in fact from two sets of clicks to four, as if punishing Pike for trying to escape by doubling.

At the next corner Pike looks for an outlet but sees instead two more sets of men coming from either side of the cross street—forcing him forward—and at the next block the same—with only one option Pike is compelled to go straight, the sound from behind him swelling—shuttling him now to the right by more men coming from his front and left—and the ever-present clicking from behind—to be herded across the city and to have the streets inundated from all sides—leaving only one route to follow—Pike breaks into a run, but the tide of those chasing him is faster—enclosing and embracing his path from all side streets at once—his lips chapped and heart racing—hundreds of charcoal suits in his wake snap in a kind of bull-baiting with Pike as their captive—umbrellas and briefcases holding got knows what—tiny syringes to make him sleep, Pike thinks—and directly ahead of him the avenue opens up onto the War Memorial—Pike and the businessmen spill out into the plaza in waves—and their charcoal suits scattering with their own individual purpose— all heading their separate directions deliberately.

There is a lone speaker in the plaza playing music, and Pike can hear its two lines of melody crashing and resonating against one another—sound waves in and out of phase—and the intermittent moments of constructive and destructive interference—even when silent, the structures are still there—in the sea of dispersing suit coats, Pike eyes a jacket of gray fur walking away from him—a squirrel-fur jacket made from hundreds of American grays, Pike imagines—a lining of the softest reds— whose tails were thrown aside and meat discarded, grilled or dried or left in the sun, and only the most velvety of bellies are cropped into small squares— sewn together like a quilt and formed into a jacket—tailored and fitted and hemmed and worn.

Pike knows that he is a fraud himself, but perhaps this man is authentic—part or patron of the American fur trade—a mountain man much like the cowboy, inexhaustible, with his jaw-traps clamping down on the paws of small mammals—his buffalo rifle poised—gathering up all the squirrels of the

Midwest and sewing them one by one into chic
fashion. The man is rooted in a history that perhaps he does not or cannot understand, and this
gives Pike some semblance of calm—to have faith
in his own ignorance—and the man stands with
an overly upright posture, walking without moving
his torso at all—his arms and legs and hips sway
in dialogue—trading positions and trading back—
while his middle appears fixed in perfect stasis.

The buildings surrounding the War Memorial are capped with copper roofs faded to a rich
green patina—weathered and made more viv-
id through wear—never fixed or stagnant—but
forming deeper greens and deeper contrasts—the
chemical reactions continue to fire, and the man
with the squirrel-fur jacket exchanges nods with
other businessmen on the plaza floor—whether innocent strangers or fellow conspirators, Pike
is unsure—though he feels a certain sympathy
for the man with the squirrel-fur jacket—he too
perhaps is being tormented by the continual itch
of a phantom limb—that during his spine cor-
rection, Pike imagines, the man with the squirrel-fur jacket had to undergo a great deal of
pain—there is a difference between those who
have experienced pain and those who haven't—
and how jealous Pike feels to see him walking

upright now and with the utmost confidence.

Pike considers the man's former versions—in high school, the social leech on others' conversations—in the hospital, the stoic in the face of excessive pain—and the man with the squirrel-fur jacket certainly has a fortune, whether it is inherited or earned or both—a food magnate wearing fur, Pike thinks—a defense contractor with a vest made up of tiny insect bodies—thorax and abdomen and reflective internal skeletons weaved into a fabric of deep grays and reds. The man moves vertically like a sine wave over the ground—with a dip in the knees and bob of the shoulders—the man with the squirrel-fur jacket shifts in and out of phase with the businessmen walking in and around the plaza.

He makes laps with the War Memorial acting as his hub—circling with a certain urgency and speed—surpassing the other pedestrians on the square and making lap upon lap—though Pike is confused by this manner of drift and aimless wandering—to have a purpose, a direction, a destination he must be following—or if he were simply exercising, it seems unlikely that the man would be wearing fur—if taking a stroll, he would not be circling with such pressing gravity—and above all else, Pike is confused by the man's pace—the

unrelenting and effortless speed of his walk—
not rushed or forced—but in long, smooth, easy
strides, the man breaks past those around him
without appearing to exert any effort, his legs
seeming to move just as quickly as the businessmen beside him, but he travels exponentially faster.

Pike feels trapped standing next to the War Memorial—fixed at the eye of the panopticon, his prison
is inverted inside out—the man circling so fast now
that Pike can nearly see the wake of his velocity—a
lasso whipped into a circle and enclosed by a porous fence of one—an electron circling its nucleus
like a cloud—and the man's individual position is
difficult to see, to freeze, to mark in space—and
Pike's sense of him boils down to probabilities—
knowing at best that he is perhaps in a particular
range or region—and Pike plots the man's suspected course forward with diminishing amounts
of certainty—a daylight apparition—unaware of
where there is open path or tragic collision—Pike
picks a firm and arbitrary line out of the square,
Rutherford's plum pudding model of the atom.

Pike does not try to time his run but simply begins moving forward—from the eye of the War
Memorial towards the circling man in the squirrel-fur jacket—he begins at a trot and proceeds

to an outright charge—the man with the squirrel-fur jacket appearing as a blur of gray and
red—pulses of air and sound hitting Pike at irregular intervals—crossing the pavers and accelerating to his maximum—Pike bites his lip as
he approaches the plane of the man's circling—a
Doppler effect shifting of experience dependent
on relative speed—and to his great surprise Pike
passes through the invisible line unscathed—no
T-boned crash—no horrible collision—and slowing his breath into shallow percussive pants, he
can see the man at the opposite end of the plaza,
having significantly reduced his relative velocity.

In Indianapolis the sky colors the city at midday—
and Pike is amazed that he has avoided immediate
and complete destruction, amazed that he is alive
at all and that the function of his body, the function of the city, doesn't arrest at any given moment,
or that it ever began working in the first place,
during a war, and Pike thinks about his own bungalow in the Broad Ripple district with two bed-
rooms and an office, a living room and kitchen—
all of the neighboring affluent hippies with their
jobs in finance—he feels nostalgic and patriotic
and wants to go home, wants to know something
clearly and cleanly—acutely aware of his limita-
tions—but Pike wants to go home—a fraud, Pike

thinks—but one who is at least relatively genuine.

In his bungalow, Pike can listen to Motown and watch television, commit complete and total blasphemy and not fear any reprisals or reproach, or do his hair like a fop and then undo it before returning to the public sphere—he is tired of being followed and watched and threatened with syringes—small patrolling armies of naval cadets and businessmen—eyes from each overhead window looking down on his every move and every false rhythm—and yet, the White Fingered Doctor is still out there in the city, conspiring against him, Pike thinks—coming for him even if he is not coming for the White Fingered Doctor—and he points himself in the direction of Broad Ripple and sets off happily and in the mode of a pilgrim—the cathedral of Santiago de Compostela—in need of a hat, perhaps, but Pike only has his white pants and brown leather shoes—his *New York Times* and his interview of Sixtus Petraeus.

On foot Pike travels three east-west blocks in exactly three hundred strides. He estimates the floor-to-floor height of the neighboring buildings in his head and converts these measurements into meters—pausing at red lights and stop signs and proceeding to cross streets only when directed by

street signs—noting the traffic in both directions
and whether there is ample time and space in order to cross the street safely—a fascination with
the banal—not that he finds it interesting per se
or that anything is interesting per se—but he finds
it interesting that Indianapolis exists in the first
place—that General David Petraeus exists—offici-
ating the opening coin flip at Super Bowl XLIII—
and how the National Football League and the
military have been in bed with each other for forty
years now—recruiting in the same moment young
men and women who enjoy both blood sport and
America—to watch *Monday Night Football* and
to join the Marine Corps—to buy a Ford F-150
and listen to *Carmina Burana*—but with no one
to place the blame upon directly, he blindly and
self-servingly walks forward on the sidewalk.

At home Pike's television receives its signal over
the airwaves via rabbit ears—Pike misses its news
coverage of celebrities, misses David Petraeus in
video form, of real and fake government agents
in strained conversation, and the division of divided parts that don't form a coherent whole, or
even an enjoyable one, but one of temporary and
fleeting distraction—with pop music covers playing outside of the department store's display window—and with a bit more wisp than the original,

Pike thinks—outliving its first use and being fully violated by another—and how wonderful—to consume and digest, to provide relief and contrast, to suspend himself within Indianapolis and within his perfectly justified sense of terror.

Pike reminds himself that he is not afraid but on his way home—not afraid of the eyes watching him from the display window—of mothers and children shopping for school supplies—not afraid of the mannequins modeling school uniforms or the Bradley Nurse and the Modular Man trying on denim Wranglers—and he cannot believe they are once again standing before him—amazed at his own sense of recall—not realizing that it is the Modular Man before stating it to himself—not realizing it is the Bradley Nurse before seeing her with the Modular Man—at least he thinks it is them—faceless, shifting, leeches—pretending not to be following him—pretending not to be watching his every move—but why else would they be there—the Bradley Nurse carrying a vial to be injected—the Modular Man even stronger than he was before—his golden section increased in size by at least one order of magnitude.

The Modular Man has a 38" waist and is perfectly proportional—the Bradley Nurse is grossly more attractive now that she is dressed as Miss Rodeo than when she was wearing her work nylon whites—having stolen the Dietrich Nurse's looks, Pike thinks—and he worries for the Dietrich Nurse—she is no match for both of them together—and in front of a mirror the Bradley Nurse has the Modular Man spin to model his new Wranglers—both of them faceless—comparing the fit and length and grip of the jeans to a pair that is one size smaller—deciding on the tighter pair—and seeming to ignore Pike entirely—paying at the register and leaving the store. They do not look at him or take any notice—walking in the opposite direction apparently so pleased with their purchases— the fiends, Pike thinks—and rather than having them double-back behind him or alert the White Fingered Doctor, Pike turns and begins to follow.

Pike wants to go home to Broad Ripple but refuses to be victimized—prodded and poked and forcibly made familiar with those he has no desire to be familiar—to be under constant surveillance and to be opened during surgery—to undergo random violence and violation without cause or explanation—Pike had not seen it before, but he realizes that the Bradley Nurse and the Modular Man are in love—or at least a kind of love—and Pike wonders whether a villain can experience love

like he feels love—the way Humbert feels love—
the way they talk close and whisper to each other
on the sidewalk—leaning in toward the other and
walking perpendicular to that lean—succeeding in
expressing affection, but completely inefficient in
terms of walking or climbing stairs—and Pike has
no problem keeping up and keeping his eyes on the
pair—close enough to know that they are speaking, but not close enough to make out their words.

The Bradley Nurse and the Modular Man smoke
Phillip Morris cigarettes and exhale in the shape
of monks and devils and amorphous clouds—the
scent of tobacco and mint reaching Pike faint-
ly—and he wishes he had a filter to wash the
oxygen that enters his own lungs—to protect
himself at least, if it isn't possible to hold out for
the public good—to resent with petty bitterness
how the Bradley Nurse and Modular Man have
found each other—it is humid in Indianapolis, and
Pike breathes in the moisture and secondhand
smoke—the airborne soot and tar affixing to his
lungs in tiny increments—on a scale that does not
have any effect and does not really matter, Pike
thinks—but it is enough that he thinks about the
process and feels good about himself—how the
Bradley Nurse breathes in deeply with ill-aban-
don—and how the Modular Man smiles—inscru-

tably smiling—and with a name like the Modular Man, god knows what he may be thinking.

At the intersection the Bradley Nurse and the Modular Man kiss goodbye and walk in separate directions—the Modular Man looking less like the Modular Man than before—in isolation harder to place or contextualize—and Pike is uncertain whether it is the Modular Man at all, or whether he is just some random cowboy that he does not care about—certainly taller than Pike, but otherwise unexceptional—and he decides to follow the Bradley Nurse who remains on foot and carries a purse under her arm—full of syringes and vials and explosive charges—Pike having read that conspirators and con men never look how you would think that they would look, and the unassuming Miss Rodeo image that the Bradley Nurse wears instills such trust and attraction that Pike knows that she must be plotting against him.

A plaid as busy as the one that the Bradley Nurse is wearing instills a deep sense of fear in Pike— preferring simple solids or stripes—though her denim Wranglers admittedly do provide a certain *essential nature* and *grounding* to the outfit—and this seems to complement the level of accident to her plaid—Pike feeling somewhat hypnotized—

her shirt and string tie, her disregard for good taste and anachronism—and the Bradley Nurse continues to walk with a sense of purpose that Pike respects—wanting to get home perhaps or to instigate some terrific injustice, to stick some innocent bystander with one of her syringes, or to circle behind Pike and begin following him—and she heel-toes her cowboy boots with the rhythm of a country song—the pulse of the radio traveling down to her feet—the music made flesh and embodied into Miss Rodeo's very way of being.

Tailing the Bradley Nurse Pike passes a military recruiting station and a flower shop where a man with a bouquet of yellows is telling his cell phone, "God this is infuriating"—and Pike agrees— though perhaps for different reasons than the man with the yellows—the Bradley nurse, even when disguised, refuses to do anything incriminating at all—perhaps showing some moral lapse in smoking her Phillip Morris cigarettes or in wearing her string tie, Pike thinks—but who can blame her— both fully intoxicating—a deep blue and turquoise lapis lazuli around her neck, absolutely charming Phillip Morris representatives, with more friends and more cigarettes and really comfortable boots— Pike begins considering the charmed life of the cowgirl smoker with a kind of fetishized glee.

In Miss Rodeo's canary-yellow bag, there are surely a number of incriminating items—and he decides that he must take it—the most certain way
of showing that Miss Rodeo is conspiring against
him—that she has arbitrarily or deliberately declared war on Pike, he thinks—or some other en-
tity where he is mere collateral damage—not even
worth consideration—and he moves up behind
her, applauding his own clandestine movement,
certain that no act so dark and so underhand-
ed could fail to prove his own righteousness—to
prove Miss Rodeo's guilt—and he jumps to a run
and grabs the canary-yellow strap of her bag—he
pulls and yanks and tries to continue running, but
there is a counter tension—Miss Rodeo failing to
let go—with a horrible sense of calm in her face.

Taller and stronger and better looking than Pike,
Miss Rodeo is unnaturally composed given that a
weak pathetic thief is attempting to take her bag,
Pike thinks—and it would be easier if she weren't
so strong or so attractive, if she weren't so confident
and weren't a real cowgirl—Miss Rodeo herself
even—and how she most likely resists the advances
of score upon score of synchronic cowboys—who
ride live bucking horses—and Pike can see the
equation in his mind with a series of greater-than

signs and Miss Rodeo at the top of the food chain—
Miss Rodeo > cowboy > bucking horse > Pike—and her
grip is invincible—where in her single hand she
has the strength of legs—great muscular legs that
are good for running away—and try as he might
Pike cannot free the canary-yellow bag from Miss
Rodeo—the two of them finding themselves at a
kind of stalemate and neither truly tugging anymore but simply holding on—standing next to one
another peaceably sharing the weight of the load.

Pike considers telling Miss Rodeo how sublime-
ly beautiful she is, but he decides against it—
that this is neither the time nor the place—and
instead he tries a final time to steal her bag with
a great lunge of his body to his immediate right
that Miss Rodeo absorbs easily—and they return
to their standstill before she begins to club Pike
on the top of the head with her free fist, club-
bing him on the shoulder and chest and back and
face—a perverse kind of blow from the side that
meets Pike squarely on the neck—and it takes
what seems like a long time for him to realize
that he should relinquish the canary-yellow bag
that is tying him to the spot—to return to Miss
Rodeo what is hers—who is now using the bag
as a kind of tether to inch him closer and keep
him there to cudgel him harder—and Miss Ro-

deo rains blow upon blow at Pike's now absent appendix, as if she knows somehow to hit him there.

Running away being the ethical choice, Pike releases his grip on the canary-yellow bag and begins to run—given that fear is justified in this circumstance as it is in most—he slaloms past the pedestrians on the sidewalk as if in a steeple chase—past an ominous black cat watching from the sidewalk whom Pike associates with *bad luck*—feeling his fate, feeling accident—his own personal failures and the status quo of discomfort and sedation—the inalienable ineptitude of his own will—always coming into being and never actually able to be—Pike inhales hard to catch his breath and looks back to see if Miss Rodeo is following him—but she isn't—and he can see only a singer-songwriter playing acoustic guitar—disgusting, Pike thinks—and to his right a crowd of furiously beautiful people all smiling—holding hands and dressed in bright reds and greens—Pike instinctively salivates at the crowd's particular shade of red—and he bites his lower lip and thinks of going home.

Beside Pike on the sidewalk, a war veteran without legs is sleeping—and how curious, Pike thinks—giving the war veteran a wide berth—placing his palms upon his middle where Miss Rodeo's blows caused him the most pain—thinking about his own bungalow and television and how he really must not dawdle because the White Fingered Doctor will soon be aware of his last known location. Already Pike can feel the swell of eyes upon him, sticking out like rot amongst the beautiful people in red, an uneasy consciousness amongst a mass of optimism—perhaps the television lied when it told him that life would work out well—or even decently—so pleasing and charming and full of good cheer—Pike breathes in the air of Indianapolis and imagines the crowd in red against a pure white background—and as if he had just taken a sedative, Pike immediately feels more calm.

*

It is hot in the sun and cool in the shade, and Pike is having a hard time regulating his own temperature, moving from block to block at a good pace, but not so fast as to attract undo attention to himself—and you can do almost anything so as long as you don't attract undo attention, Pike thinks—and this, perhaps, was his failure in his attempt to accost Miss Rodeo—how you should never call too much attention to yourself in circumstances such as these, where Pike's anonymity is paramount and with so many eyes upon him—or when he is alone or feels that he is alone, or when he does not know who may or may not be watching. Pike thinks about where Miss Rodeo and the Modular Man might be meeting again and with what motive—how they will plot against him and tell the White Fingered Doctor how Pike had failed and was beaten—and how he still has no proof that they are conspiring against him—beyond the indisputable fact that they most certainly are.

Faith, Pike thinks, both paranoid and secular is healthy for one's soul. He is not one for false hope or false modesty, Pike tells himself, but a tyrannical interrogating check that leaves the empirical world raw—and this is where Pike likes it— the kind of immediate and universal pleasure of having one's back scratched—if it was only that simple—and if only they would let him be and stop following him—if only he could accept being victimized and simply take it—unconscious of his surroundings, Pike has walked clear up to the War Memorial and its rising limestone monolith—with a jolt and a scream—he scolds himself for calling such attention to himself—for failing to recognize where he is going or what might be coming out of his mouth—uncertain whether he has been speaking only in his head or vocalizing all of his thoughts for anyone and everyone to hear.

Pike is uncertain whether he has just said the words *David Petraeus* only in his mind or out loud for the spies around him—it is particularly disconcerting because sitting at the base of the War Memorial is the Secondary Doctor dressed in white—at least it looks like the Secondary Doctor—and Pike knows of the Secondary Doctor's fondness for Petraeus—knows of his allegiance to the White Fingered Doctor—and dear god, Pike thinks—the Secondary Doctor is so incredibly clean—how can he get his hands disinfected after doing what he does with his hands—how do his clothes stay so white and his face so clean shaven—he is smoking a cigarette but even that seems virtuous—and he is so attractive and shines up so nicely that Pike does not trust him at all—uncertain whether he has snuck up on the Secondary Doctor or whether he is being baited in—and feeling impelled to follow as the Secondary Doctor walks away from the memorial, Pike leaves his seat knowing full well that it may be a trap.

Pike scans the windows on the street and looks for eyes that may be watching—he has seen enough cowboy movies to know the way that an ambush works and the importance of the high ground—though it seems quiet, and this disturbs Pike even

more—following the white jacket of the Secondary Doctor into a convenience store where
he buys nothing and leaves—continues walking
down the street, and Pike continues to follow—
idling in front of a brick structure before carrying
on—pausing at a side street and standing completely still and completely silent, as if his body
has turned to stone, refusing to make any sound
or make any movement—doing nothing at all—
as if that were ever possible—and Pike watches
the Secondary Doctor and watches more closely.

The Secondary Doctor stands still, without any
idle or purposeful drive. He does nothing for a
time that Pike has difficulty quantifying—and
Pike wonders whether the Secondary Doctor's
heart has stopped or whether he is still breathing—wonders if his thoughts have gone black or
just his body—with no conspiracy or syringe or
surgical mask—but like death, a clear conscience,
or a complete lack of one—Pike looks for any
trace or residual point of life—begins to worry as
he widens his field of view, and it is not just the
Secondary Doctor but everyone on the street—
frozen and solidified—terrifying in their complete
lack of threat—Pike forces himself to walk for fear
of becoming frozen himself—he walks up to the
Secondary Doctor and looks at him in the eyes

and in the mouth—looks at his warm motionless
face—and Pike accelerates to a run and moves as
fast as he can away from those not chasing him.

Pike passes man upon man frozen on the street—a
field of stationary mannequins modeling jeans and
cowboy plaids—their syringes and vials—Pike
weaves between the crowd and feels repelled by
each isolated peg—the polar ends of a magnet—
pushed and pulled away in an orbit of inverse gravity. Pike moves faster, but the mannequins spread
in great fields, and perhaps he was better off standing next to the Secondary Doctor and limiting his
scope to a horrifying one rather than realizing the
scale of it all—wondering if it is the same in Broad
Ripple—the same in the boilermaker's residential
district—stopping to breathe in the air through
his nose—and lurching to life, the mannequins
once again begin moving—slowly at first—
and then returning back to the pace of the city.

The porous crowds swarm, and Pike takes in the
information around him—they are far too numer-
ous to count or track or lay his hands upon—circling him like expendable gnats in a smokescreen
of false positives or false memories—Nat Turner
cutting into his side—Pike cannot take it all in at
once, but only a fraction—the furiously beautiful

people in red and the cheery people in green—enlivened back to life after nearly freezing to death, and failing to realize their own proximity to permanent stasis—to be fragile or hardhearted—Pike wonders how he will ever be able to tell the true spies from the low-level operators placed there by the White Fingered Doctor as foils or diversions—not the isolated conmen among innocents, but the true villains among a sea of minor thieves.

Pike believes that on the whole, true villains are generally taller and more attractive than minor thieves—and perhaps this is one litmus test that may be telling, Pike thinks—that they generally wear more yellows and blues and whites and plaids—and fewer reds, greens, pastels, and neons—but then there are exceptions and provisos, and it is terribly difficult to tell—the villains are so cagey and sharp that they blend in amongst the crowd—and rather than singling out the Alsatian, the Modular Man, or whatever shifting devil should enter his path—Pike decides to shoot brown into the thick of them—they are all working for the White Fingered Doctor anyway—whether they know they are working for the White Fingered Doctor or not—regardless, they are responsible and deserve what's coming to them—Pike hunting antelope on the Serengeti and watching for the straggling, sick, or wounded, to pick off from the back of the herd.

To Pike's right, the Rainbow Girl is just over four feet tall and wears pastels—a sure tipoff that she is not a true villain, Pike thinks—but she walks by herself in uniform, passing encoded messages back and forth imprinted on her contact lenses, carrying an assortment of blades in her purse—an assassin—and the White Fingered Doctor is surely using her for something—the White Fingered Doctor who is nothing if not efficient—willing to deploy all resources necessary, and reportedly having such a capacity as to play dozens of games of chess simultaneously—all blind and in his head like Luzhin—and winning each time—that yes, Pike thinks—the White Fingered Doctor would not squander a resource like the Rainbow Girl— surely she has been put to work like the others, and Pike walks beside her and begins inching the Rainbow Girl towards the edge of the sidewalk, as if he is running a car slowly off of the road.

"Excuse me," the Rainbow Girl says—and a quiet, meek *excuse me* it is too, soft and not accusatory— an honest inquiry and not forced inquisition—per- haps the Rainbow Girl is a truth seeker too—and this strikes a chord in Pike, softens and melts him, so much so that he kicks himself for being so weak and taken in by her deception—and the Rainbow Girl isn't innocent at all—she isn't even a common thief, but a villain deserving of punishment—a victory at last—Pike firing out at random and capturing one of the White Fingered Doctor's chief lieutenants—the mere thought of which makes him want to eat red meat—he does not answer her calls, but calmly waits for a side street—walks beside the Rainbow Girl until the avenue opens up onto another—ignoring her repeated *excuse me's*.

At the mouth of the intersection Pike turns to address the Rainbow Girl and inches her back off of the main avenue—questioning her about the contents of her bag, what she know about the White Fingered Doctor, the operation, the Modular Man—questions spilling out of Pike with no hope for an answer—and the Rainbow Girl, frightened but keeping her calm, takes her mace out of her purse and sprays Pike full in the nose, mouth, and eyes—sucking in the aerosol and feeling an instinctive suffocation—blinded and tearing up—Pike hears the soft patter of the Rainbow Girl's jellies running away—his hopes for information and truth evading him—and the Rainbow Girl is a savage and a brute, Pike thinks—and clearly the White Fingered Doctor has no intention of loosing control, no intention of shifting the balance of power.

Suffering and suffering alone, Pike wraps himself up and favors his face and abdomen. He finds the gutter on his hands and knees and washes his eyes in a still puddle—where perhaps some of the spray is coming out, Pike thinks, but god knows what else coming in—the paranoid faith of compromise—there is no clean option, but all of them filthy—and Pike forces himself to mechanically cry to clear his vision—tear after tear with no emotional weight behind it, but simply his body recovering and needing rest—with the sun full overhead, even deep within the side street is sunny—and Pike lies in the light for what seems like days thinking of his home in the Broad Ripple district—how at least hardly any of his neighbors have children—and thank god for that Pike thinks—imagining them screaming in their wallowing holes and swimming like trash in the rain.

Pike shuffles back to the main avenue where the people in red are swarming—crowds of savage thieves ignoring Pike—performing their individual tasks with individual purpose—the morally base, Pike thinks—taking their orders from above and poised to strike at any shout or acceleration to violence—uncertain whether the tribe will turn against them—in his frustration Pike finds some internal satisfaction in lashing out at those who do not understand—calling them frauds right to their faces—and if only he could find any clear statement of fact or identify the right question to ask—feeling the forces from outside of himself, but not knowing how to respond—terrified both irrationally and rationally, and not knowing how to distinguish the one from the other.

Pike's eyes fill and refill with fluid. At regular intervals he wipes them clean with his hands— hands just as filthy as the Secondary Doctor's that had entered his belly—working his way down the sidewalk through the crowd of beautiful people in a jagged line—Pike's sight, smell, and sense of balance are helpless to the White Fingered Doctor's advances—his inner ear having lost its pressure—surrounded by threat—and by now the Rainbow Girl has certainly reported his last known location, Pike thinks—gathered them all together to decide his fate without consulting him. Pike slouches on the sidewalk and looks up at those watching him from above— thinking how hideous he must look—his white pants and brown leather shoes—his foreshortened body and his face in shadow—and he points himself once again in the direction of Broad Ripple and walks slowly and assertively in that direction.

In Indianapolis, everyone walks and no one drives automobiles. Pike matches the pace of a war veteran and a mother of two—whose children fail to maintain any consistent trajectory but punctuate their movement with fits of intense focus and slow distraction—the savages, Pike thinks—and he looks to the windows overlooking the street to see who may be looking down at him, looks down each side street with a cold apprehension as he passes—a deep anxiety meeting him at each approaching marker on the grid, and relief when he fails to see the Modular Man or the White Fingered Doctor coming for him—when he feels their absence—or when he fails to see the Bradley Nurse threatening with syringe in hand—Pike's fear recycles with each subsequent block, and the blocks seemingly stretch on without end—Broad Acre City or Ville Radieuse—to privilege the grid first and topography second—Pike knows that they must be out there somewhere—and he wipes his eyes to see more clearly—his tears well up, and he wipes them clear again.

Pike tells himself that he is not irrational or mad—emotional or pathetic—his tears functioning upon instinct—input and response—and the body can't help it when the world is the way that it is—when the Rainbow Girl lashes out at him, or when he is followed and beaten and universally frowned upon—called mad and a villain by those certainly madder and more villainous—his tears, Pike tells himself, are purely utilitarian—to wash out the salt scales coating his lenses—the White Fingered Doctor's influence seeping through tiny invisible pores—and Pike sees a man walking with his spaniel along the sidewalk slowly—the dog carries a stick that is the length of her body, extended like a cantilever out from her jaws—panting happily and craning her neck to compensate for the weight—the tiny dog and the branch hanging from her mouth, gigantic.

Pike looks in the direction of Broad Ripple and looks at the man with the spaniel. In the baiting heat, the man with the spaniel, and the spaniel herself, breathe in the humid air of Indianapolis with their mouths wide open—waiting for an opportunity to pierce his back with their needles, Pike thinks—to report his location to the White Fingered Doctor for being too conspicuous and attracting too much undo attention. Pike cannot turn his back on them—but needs to be silent or more intelligent, to stand completely still—to sneak up close to the man with his spaniel and lurch and reel—and Pike

is forced to follow them so that they cannot follow him—the man continuing down the street on
the sidewalk, and Pike turns deliberately to follow.

Pike plays a game with himself while walking—
fixing his eyes on someone far out in front of him,
on one side of the street or another, and attempts
to hold and trace them all of the way past his
hip—but always, he loses them within the crowd
or the background as his eyes slip from side to
side, and glazing over are unable to return with
any confidence to their source—passed off and
mistaken—or limited to within the general area
of, Pike thinks—he chooses a window overlooking
the street with yellow curtains—a tiny diorama of
Midwestern life—but with a blink Pike is uncertain as to whether he is still looking at the same
window or the one adjacent to it, whether the curtains are same shade of yellow—and on the street
the man with the spaniel bleeds out into larger
and larger spheres of possibility—Pike calculating
the rate of the man's velocity and the likelihood
that he has reached a particular point—a street
sign, a corner, a crack in the sidewalk—having
fixed his eyes upon him and having never let him
go—but never able to see him from the front—
to be able to stare down his face and to see his
tiny ivory teeth smiling—Pike wonders whether

he is still the same man as he was just a moment ago—whether he is the same as the man he saw leaving the pub—smoke rising from behind it.

Down the length of the median a row of poplars bloom. Spherical greens resting upon trunks of calcified bark—its skin like dried scabs—and if a branch were to break and the tree still had a voice, Pike thinks—it would be certain to rush out bleeding and in shouts of pain. He tails the man with the spaniel along the sidewalk and below the anonymous window glass—the Indianapolis skyline, like its residents, indistinguishable from any other city—its sisters in the International Style—undaunted by the same worn tracks across the sky—Pike imagines bringing the sun down low like Phaëthon and scorching the earth permanently—and whether to risk disaster or to strike him dead by lightning—Pike moves cautiously from a distance—it is safer from a distance with the spaniel bounding and pulling the leash taut around her neck—with each great onrush, the greater the restriction of her throat—her smiles and panting—Pike has never seen before a happier or more contented spaniel.

They travel in a line through shade and under the filtering iridescent leaves. The street plan,

etched into the ground, multiplies and is extrud-
ed into three dimensions—the rising rectilinear
steel-framed towers and the odd sloped or mansard roof—there is no accounting for taste, Pike
thinks. There are no hills in Indianapolis, but in
line together they trace the contours of a soft low-
set rise—a swale of glacial sediment, or a once
agricultural edge—where the plows stopped and
fields turned into subdivisions—the sand fixed
into place by grasses and paved over—Pike can see
rows upon rows of new houses, neighbors mirroring neighbors, immature saplings in circular beds
and dragon teeth planted deep into the earth so
as to sprout up in the form of soldiers. On one
end of the street, Pike sees a trampoline, and on
the other end, an identical trampoline—it is the
same along each subsequent parallel line—the
spaniel leading the way by tugging at her leash—
somehow recognizing home amidst the indistinguishable grid and she tugs harder—a left turn
and then another left—and they must be close.

Overhead, two white jet streams crisscross the
sky—white on blue—one traveling north and the
other west—Pike circling heliotropic with the sun
at solar noon—striving and telling himself that he
must be striving—blown away by a captive wind—
not to Broad Ripple and home—but to an area

that looks just like it—as if to be authentic matters somehow. The man turns onto a smaller road past the stone entryway of a subdivision with paired black obelisks on either side of the street running parallel to an open drainage ditch—marked by a mulberry tree with its red berries pulsing blood as if from a water pipe—"Come Glen," the man says to the spaniel, who busies herself with the ground—tracing a scent perhaps that marks the way invisibly—and Pike can hear the spaniel's name being called—just close enough to overhear—and finally, he has found the right distance between them.

The house is a one-story Usonian with a flat roof and clearstory windows—part of the landscape to hide themselves—plane upon flat plane—and built on a budget for the middle classes without attics or closets to hide their sedatives—those to make you go to sleep so as to dream, and those that place you just before dream in delirium—to run out from the canvas of the painting. This is how the enemy lives, Pike thinks—always back to business in the Midwest with no need to hide because everyone is disaffected—the long undifferentiated horizon and the absence of any juxtaposition—always tuning one's head and returning to the task at hand. The man pauses before the mulberry tree to pick a berry and tosses it haphazardly towards a stop sign, and they are up and moving without waiting to hear or see if it has hit its mark—walking to the front of the Usonian and disappearing inside— the spaniel's bark muted—missile silos hiding in plain sight in corn fields—and Pike thinks of his home in Broad Ripple and how the White Fingered Doctor must be lying in wait for him there.

From the yard, the central bay window frames the man's kitchen table—porcelain dishes of a pristine white filled with lettuce wraps for dipping—behind them paintings on the wall depicting paired golden labradors with mallards in their mouths— making sacrifices to some other god, Pike thinks— burning a hecatomb of bulls so that the battle turns out right. The man disappears out of view and returns to pat the spaniel behind the ears—offering her bits of lamb and she licks his fingers clean—he spoons out dish after dish onto his plate before taking his own seat—and it is safer behind glass, Pike thinks—as in a zoo or an aquarium—to have him contained within and to avoid being overrun inside the man's natural habitat—reading his newspaper and glancing up to transfer food safely into his mouth. Pike wonders if the man is reading the interview of Sixtus Petraeus—wonders what the man was doing outside of the frame of the window— some nefarious act no doubt—and what the stakes are of eating lunch, idyllic, with a dog at his feet.

The man sits motionless like a still life of fruit decaying. His glass is filled with white wine, and the reflective glint of the lamp paints the dead fish eyes that stare up at Pike in their absent deliberation—for what it means to rest upon this table without eyelids and to be forced to stare—forced unwillingly even when dead to take in the sight of the man chewing. Pike swats at a mosquito in the center of the yard—the street sounds collapsing upon him from either side—the backyard pool's splash and the stereo trampoline springs—shouts of joy and shouts of suppressed pain posing as joy—Pike is unable to parse the window tableau from the sound of the trampoline stretching—the shouts from the neighbor's pool of either lust or drowning—and the spaniel's ever-observant bark batting at the window glass with both paws—one sound mixing with another—the cicada drone of the hospital and the television white. Pike can only freeze as the man rises from the table to peer out at him through the window. The man walks towards the inner glass and cups his hands like great eyebrows to block out the glare. It was self-defense, Pike thinks—trying to identify the distortion of the man's face— Darwin's *The Expression of the Emotions in Man and Animals*—confusion, despair, rage, anguish.

Pike imagines home with a clarity he has not felt for some time—though he senses no concrete images or thoughts—fixed in the present with his brown shoes on the green lawn—the bay window now empty. The man having exited the frame has turned the room once again to still life: the same decaying food, the kind eyes of statuary, the dead blank stares of fish eyes—at least these can be counted on. Perhaps the man had recognized him from before or that he had been marked somehow for the spaniel to track—marked invisibly, so that they are always able to find him—and with a metallic click—the man with the spaniel emerges from the front door of the Usonian—the sound of the pool and the trampoline spring—and not knowing what else to do besides run, Pike hustles down the road towards the stone entryway—pulled backwards with each stride and each identical house—the tunnel accelerating—and on either side of him the same kaleidoscopic facade is turned and refracted upon different mirrored plans—the same house in lighter or darker shades of river stone—again and again—and faster with each realization of delay and each incremental unit of fear—Pike passing the paired obelisks. Patron saint protect me.

*

Pike wakes to the sound of water dripping—estuaries of brackish salt and brine—the seashore of Middle America mirrored in the White River running through Indianapolis and making its way south to the Ohio and west to the Mississippi—never wide or deep enough to serve as the artery the city's founder's once thought it would be, and here, not much more than a drainage ditch. In the distance between what Pike believed would be and what would become reality—to see his insides fail and to be stalked and followed and bruised facedown in the grass—Pike's eyes have trouble holding their focus upon any whole frame at any one time—between what is close and what is far away—the lines of fiber and fill rise from their roots and each tiny stalk of grass—a cancer, Pike thinks—that in sum makes a neat bed for his head to rest on. He is not in pain but has no memory of the past minutes or hours—surveying his imprint in the field and the surrounding sightlines—unable to make out the subdivision or War Memorial or any perusing dogs—and beside him, the persistent drip from an open pipe—acid or solvent—finding its way into the water table.

If he had been stuck from behind, Pike imagines, there would be more clear physical marks—a tear

of metal on flesh, perhaps, or the submersion of
sound wrapping his inner ear like cellophane and
the distancing and torqueing of time, much less
his own sense of balance, into some new alternative normal—conned by some Jane Addams
philanthropist or Bill Thompson strong-arm into
believing that only the dishonest can govern the
unethical, and that one should never hold onto
one's pacifism when the world has already decided
to go to war. Pike never knows when he is being
conned anyway, he thinks—because he believes
them from the first—like faith or the IV in the
hospital—not a con at all but a conduit for god
knows what chemicals or constrictions, drugs of
slow release, which might explain for the absence
of any tangible marks. How can I account for this
lack of physical violence, Pike thinks. If he were
struck from the front, then surely he would remember the Modular Man rising from the grass
reciting *Thanatopsis*—the White Fingered Doctor
with a horse bit in his hand—how great things
are born either out of necessity or raw selfish
greed—the *Ars Magna or Liber de Ludo Aleane*—
and how Cardano formulated probability simply
because he wanted to become a better gambler.

On the leeward side of the earth berm where
Pike rests, the city turns a darker green—unnat-

ural oases of topography and fairway—and in the distance, the great concrete oval where Doppler swells rise and fade to explode in shared gasped silences—a swirling Charybdis of exhaust and pain—and the incessant, mechanical circling inwards—to slam headlong into steel to cheers, or escape to drunk placid ambivalence. I can read this prophecy easily enough, Pike thinks. Some kind of disease: erysipelas, dyspepsia, jaundice, brain fever—the difference between being equally susceptible to disaster and disaster actively seeking you out—the disillusionment of the privileged surprised by any soft hardship, and the inherently susceptible crippled by their own instincts and by chance—classical conditioning and ancestral grudges generations deep—forces, magnetic or quantum, that teaches one to shoot first and ask questions later, and then to become fully self-hating for being formed in the image of something almost as awful as yourself—to hate and to hate more that one never had a choice in the matter—and seeing the contradiction only fuels Pike's synapses to speed their firing—watching a pair of birds tear at each other in the sky—some augur's vision of triumph, or the magnifying forces of spheres acting within spheres, shaming Pike in his inability to do otherwise.

There is no safety in surrender but a ceaseless gasping for air—some life insurance algorithm might tell him otherwise, Pike imagines—to consider all of the possibilities and potential risks factored over an ever-increasing expanse of time—where the probability of failure rises with each heartbeat that successfully avoids death, and without the reassurance even that if one point or tissue should fail it does not prevent another from doing so. Along the road—a white pickup pulls beside him as Pike stares into the drainage ditch with his hands in his pockets. The industrial runoff, or what Pike imagines to be runoff, forms into a thin stream past his shoes, and the wire fence extends for miles behind him—foreground to background—straight through to the speedway—and Pike only notices now what has some immediate use-value for or against him. He is caught, and he hangs his head low like a child trying to sustain some necessary absence known only to him.

"Are you all right? Do you need a ride?" the man from the pickup asks. The couple is sexless—amateur New Yorkers with gaped mouths and clear skin, with uncanny silhouettes, not of any active presence, but the remains of something greater that has been carved away—a single piece of granite infinite in its possibility, turned into woebegone animal topiary with lush ears and a sickly-brown caved in stomach. Pike walks to the cab as the man in the passenger's seat allows him to slide into the middle along the bench. New Yorkers, Pike thinks—their arrogant self-importance and profoundly good taste—their snide guilt-tripping generosity. Though the couple, in fact, says that they are from Paducah and have only driven up for the weekend race and the Blue Angel flyovers— thoughts of the Dietrich Nurse surging back in upon Pike—and how the couple's windshield is spotless like the hospital glass and how people who travel nowhere care so much about the upkeep of their vehicles—surely having just washed away the dead insects that had collected on the drive up through the Ohio River Valley—their consoles are stocked with cured meat and high fructose corn syrup—overgrown and uncoordinated—expanding too fast and orphaned from any shared history but consumption and the blind self-confidence to drive 50 miles per hour in a 25 mile-per-hour zone.

Pike sits with his hips at a distance just far enough away from grazing the couple's respective bodies on either side of him—the tiny buffer of air between them is charged with an inhumanity that is almost worse than touching—Boyle's law of pressure and volume—where one side of the bench is balanced, equal and opposite, against that of the other. Pike can feel when he is getting too close—the flirtation of their clothing—denim to khaki—awful combinations and mixings in which his mind does not want to take part—where negatives become positive—and what in fact is has nothing to do with any local desire. To deny, Pike thinks, is the same as calling things into being—to suppress, forcing him to live with the realization that the couple must be just as uncomfortable sitting next to him as he is to them.

Always Hasten Slowly, the pickup's bumper sticker had read, and from the rearview, an icon of St. Jude hangs down towards Pike's knees. Both the man and the woman wear magnetic copper bracelets to ease arthritic pain, and Pike can sense the rush of blood running from his frontal lobes down to his legs and fists—his pulse increasing along with his consciousness of touch—the base of his back against the seat rest—the pressure of each acceleration heightened and heightening—his posture too upright and his dress too disheveled—the glowing gages in the pickup's console building steadily with each rev of the engine. They ask him where they might take him, and whether he would like to use their phone—did his car break down, they ask—questioning in the kindest way possible, without speaking to it directly, how Pike might have found himself prostrate on the side of the road against the back fence of the speedway—"Broad Ripple please," Pike mumbles as if he were in a taxi, answering the first question while ignoring all others, and wondering if in the hospital they had used any heroic measures upon him—whether his heart ever stopped beating, and if so for how long.

In the pickup the couple talks across Pike—perhaps to him as well, he thinks—though he takes no notice of what they might be saying. Inside, he feels only his acute thirst—how he does not know when he might have eaten or had anything to drink last—and once called to mind, Pike is suddenly insatiable—to burn like Poliphilo or Tantalus and to ignore all sense of propriety— he grabs at the couple's soda resting on the dash and drinks it in long draughts—the conditioned air is calming—the fan and hypnotic road sounds meld into a synthetic hum—numbing all the unscripted accidents to dull bumps, Pike thinks— and a far cry from the pointed syncopation of real-life walking outside—of being in the world. There is a sense of safety within the hermetically sealed cab. The pickup merges onto the expressway, and the skyline comes into fuller view—more familiar somehow from a greater distance and behind glass—One Indiana Square—the ideal

and the unreal—the defining silhouette of Indianapolis—identical to any other office tower in
any other city—and how easy it is, Pike thinks,
to move along the expressway and successfully
avoid all of those who are trying to find him out.

From the safety of the cab, Pike interprets hiero-
glyphs off of billboards—*Do whatever you like, just
not in public*—*Patience is the ornament, guardian,
and protector of life*—though Pike doubts his ability to understand and interpret with so much information to sort and his concerted disregard for
others' autonomy and worldview. Pike's eyes play
tricks on him attempting to parse one stalk or
tree or pedestrian from another—blurred to ochre
brown—each sightline indistinguishable from the
next. On one side of the highway, office towers
playact at being a major American city—on the
other, fields of corn offer up the means of production—Broad Acre City realized, Pike thinks—
with a short drive from their offices downtown
to the fields where crops are grown—the factory refining steel—all along the same abandoned
piece of highway where they can leave you for
dead—and with no need to leave Ithaca to find
some life-killing drug—but it is all within minutes
from home—the romance of it—and Pike reels
backwards and sinks deep within the seat leather.

Content to be wrong—the couple disregards Pike's manner and dress and raw Animalia. As with many Midwesterners, it is with a willful naiveté that they assume better of Pike than he deserves and more than has been presently earned, stoically bearing the consequences of holding the benefit of the doubt and consoling themselves in their disappointment with their own private self-pity—hardened not in faith, but a blindness to all ills—and where their own flaws are met with a similar sidestepping—never to admit a bitterness directly, but rather, to massage its symptoms with not untrue kindnesses—a hollow and benevolent self-deception—not exactly a lie, Pike thinks, but a cultural ethic of self-denial and generosity, so that in spite of the inconvenience and any real concern for the outcome, the couple begins the drive thirty miles out of their way to take Pike back home. It is not with any desire to do good, but with the belief that they are the kind of people who would do good if given the opportunity, and as the pickup passes the Chase and OneAmerica Towers, Pike can see the great oxbow in the White River signaling that it is a good place to stop—where the water slows and the city follows and Broad Ripple sprouts up along this section of its banks.

Pike can feel the road sounds slow and shift to a lower cadence, off of the main throughway and onto the suburban streets—the air of the intake fan moves from filter to lungs to blood vessel capillaries—sorted and weaned down, so that at the moment of transfer—the first and only molecule available is the one that is already used up by the couple breathing to either side of Pike—full of diseases no doubt. He is not a hypochondriac, Pike thinks, but simply self-aware—how any acute happening has already happened—how eleven people have died in the industrial accident, the radio tells him—and "How terrible," the woman says shaking her head with no discernable affect that it is actually terrible—unmoved—and yet, it is exhausting to be moved all of the time, Pike thinks—afraid of both past and present—how there is no one time fixed in isolation, but it is always split between that which fades and that which is so uncertain—with nothing at center but the transient moment scanning his surrounds. Pike is glad to be enclosed inside the pickup and glad to be transient—to face one's shame alone and grateful not to show it—a purgatory of the body—its ache and recovery—consumed by the sound of the cars passing—the sound of the pickup passing others—pockets of vacuumed air released with a rush—a blue Ford Taurus—and the emptiness behind it.

Depressing the brake, the woman pulls to the side of the road and stops. Without knowing how he got there, Pike finds himself on his own street in front of his neighbor's Arts and Crafts style home. He must have told them his address at some point, Pike supposes—though he does not remember doing so—though at least his unremembered self had the good sense not to give them his real address, but that of his neighbor's—willing to take credit where no credit is due. Or perhaps they had known all along where to take him—the neighbor's beam-for-beam reconstruction of the Stickley farmhouse where she had grown up in New Jersey—importing an aesthetic from where there is no culture—its cedar shingles and Mansard roof—Pike questions whether or not to trust the absences of his memory. There is no telling what else Pike might have told them, and he feels an anxious tearing at his incapacity to act and not to act—to dry out like potash his salt and heavy metals—and to be left with only his unbearable thirst.

The neighboring house is oriented east-to-west upon the lot and not north-to-south like its model original. Red, white, and cork oaks punctuate the street, and the lawns, one after another, in squares of green provide the appearance of control, a ve-

neer for cutting down the weak and pliable and
ignoring the cracking freeze-thaw of violence.
"Take care and good luck to you," the man says.
"It'll all work out," the woman says. In the wake
of the pickup—Pike is left alone. "No one wants
your armchair philosophy," Pike says in the direction of their rear bumper—and what exactly is
going to *work out*, Pike thinks—and what exactly could the couple possibly speak to when they
are scarcely aware of the damage that has already
been done—the patronizing pats on the head and
thin distribution of platitudes posing as novelties
or complete works of art. There are gaps in Pike's
memory that he cannot seem to set right—how
there must have been a moment when he told the
couple his address, but the sound of it is all wrong.
Sure honey, he imagines the woman saying—kindly and soft spoken—to be told something abstract
or undefined—and even if it is a lie or an absence
that marks its starting point, it is this absence that
gives voice to what Pike does not want to hear.

The yard is vibrant—the neighbor's violets, common
dogs and downy yellows, that form a thin dotted
line before the hedgerow that divides the two prop-
erties—closer—not dots but paired concave sets of
wings. Let me invent a confession, Pike thinks—
one set to deceive and spoken in a church behind a

screen so that it has all of the resonant effects—to apologize for not being able to hold still and for acting upon the orders of others. When the right action is always the one that defers responsibility, no one is tied directly and no one is responsible— but passing it forwards or backwards—distanced by an order that forces one to commit—or another that digs their hands into the victim and surrenders their envelope—Pike feels fixed in between and in infinite regress. Actors—the lowest sorts of people, pretending to be someone else—they are the most egotistical of all. On stage—saying the same thing night after night, driving between the same two points, back and forth, day in and day out—or standing with a rifle in hand watching the same bits of sand erode—Pike knows, and has always known, the outcome beforehand—determined by some future tense to simply carry it out.

On one side of the farmhouse, a window has moved. Pike is sure of it. On the second floor, a window that was not there before now overlooks his yard with a clear view, like that from the Dallas Book Depository, straight into his living room. Punched into the wall or skirted and stretched from another point on the same facade, even solids are not fixed, Pike thinks—he has seen it before—the shifting and interchangeable high rises

along Meridian—empty and filled—blue to yellow—scanning both sides of the street to see who
might be watching from above. They were there,
he knows—sensing their absence without ever
having to have seen it directly—and to Pike's confession—the priest recommends to undergo some
minor penance—one that might take some fifteen
minutes of his time, when he has tried for hours
and days to free himself of it. Pike imagines con-
fessing to even greater sins that he has not committed—and the larger the transgression the better—and the braver he will be for facing it—with
all of the benefits and none of the tax of real sins—
whatever he is called upon to do in recompense,
he is not actually required to do it, because there is
no transgression in the first place. When it comes
to false positives—*I understand*, the priest would
say—and opening the front door of the farmhouse—"Good day," the neighbor calls to him.

Her inflection lands somewhere between a question and wretched imperative—in her eager,
self-conscious search for affirmation—and an at
once dismissive, guarded, imperious pride—the
neighbor knows the answer already and is in fact
sneering at whatever little Pike could add to the
conversation—how it is indeed beautiful, and how
sad that seems sometimes—but only a closed loop

and dead end is offered—and only that much because he is the only one there. The neighbor is in
fact speaking to no one at all, or only to herself,
Pike thinks—muttering under one's breath on the
city sidewalk so that people will assume the worst
of you and leave you alone—within her hardline,
self-righteous hostility, and failure to admit any
fault—not the worst of herself, but a readymade
self-sabotage laid out for Pike—and the concerted demand that he should always assume the best
of her kindnesses. She does not leave her porch
to greet him but stands at its edge as if held behind an invisible line—the single stepped cement riser off of the ground plane divides space
and holds them at a distance like dogs or children
who busy themselves constructing and violating
the human barriers that they are told not to cross.

Her voice strikes him with the impulse that he
should confess something at once—but what, Pike
thinks—or that he should bear hard to one side
and stagger backwards over dried leaves—where
each step awakens a silence that cracks and breaks
and splits in two. A car drives past them. A beetle lying flat on its back flutters all of its thousand
legs in a fury and opens its wings to right itself
again, and the neighbor smiles as Pike imagines
his confessor might in simultaneous judgment and

forgiveness of all wrongdoing. Pike waves back in the disguise of a selective forgetting. "Good day," the neighbor says again—and Pike is taken back to the operating table—to that which he could not possibly remember—and the sunflowers in his own yard raise their heads haplessly just over the hedgerow in the same shade of yellow that marked the way west—planted by those first pioneers for others to follow—annuals that die but leave plenty of seeds to grow in their place—like a variable Brigham Young's traveling east from Nauvoo to Indianapolis and not west out to Zion—to circle inward and back—Indianapolis is a good place to be from but not actually be, Pike thinks—a good place to travel through behind glass or from above, to look down on squares of tamed green and gold in a tidal pool, the copper roof's turquoise patina.

Pike wonders why the neighbor does not strike— perhaps she is confined to her porch for all time watching from her window down into Pike's bungalow and considering what it's like to be alone. The house has changed—Pike is sure of it. Its shingles, sun-beaten and blanched, were built by hand—not by any machine, designed to make it look like it was made by hand, as if that mattered somehow, mimicking all of the tiny human imperfections and accidents and reducing their neces-

sary striving to quaint decorative knickknacks—
as the roof tiles oxidize to some deeper blue and
lesser green—holding on to some inner need to
stand fast and at once apologize for the very fu-
tility of trying. There is value, Pike thinks, in the
effort expended to travel to nowhere, to return to
the same point where no one is waiting for you,
but for those lying in wait disguised to ensnare and
entrap you there. "Are you okay, Mr. Pike? Why
don't you come inside," the neighbor says. "Get
yourself something to drink. Put your feet up." If
he did not know it before, Pike knows now that
she too is not to be trusted—her good Midwestern
hospitality, her assumptive distancing politeness—
to dash Pike upon some wretched inglorious end
or otherwise die without anyone noticing—to be
the sole person holding on and branded as crazy,
but in point of fact, perfectly justified in being so.

Pike follows at a distance as the neighbor leads
him forward—entering the farmhouse, Pike
imagines his own—its textures and tectonics and
the way that sound jumps from the walls on the
main level and deadens into muffled starts below grade—not an architecture to prevent one
from dying but a document for marking finite
time—his collected ticket stubs and rabbit-eared
television—his copy of John Dewey on *habit* and

The Hypnerotomachia Poliphili that begins with a dream. The neighbor leads him through the entryway into the kitchen—oversized decorative utensils adorn the walls and tiny stacked ramekins the shelves—Pike is only able to picture objects and not space—a glass of water in a void—the neighbor's voice disembodied—talking, singing, hypnotically calling him forward or casting out lines to pull him back—exhaustion takes him— and he can hear the clicking of quick steps from behind and the sound of his own body collapse in a huddle—somehow perceiving his fall both from far away and painfully close at once—as if he were simultaneously inside and outside of himself— and how one sound must have preceded the other, Pike thinks—though he does not know which, or whether his neighbor was coming to his aid, or that it was she who struck him down from behind.

In confession, Pike feels a wounding flatness. To be still is a sickness, he thinks—and it is no longer enough to be forgiven for wrongdoings he did not commit. Pike imagines himself crying in order to split himself in two and discard the lesser half. The room in which he wakes is one of ideal domesticity—pens and quilts and sepia photographs of the neighbor as a young girl—photographs in full color of her faceless husband and faceless child—and a trio of long muzzled Afghan hounds guarding the door like Cerberus. The radio tells him that they have taken those injured in the industrial accident to the downtown hospital where the White Fingered Doctor will undoubtedly do them incalculable harm—to do to them what has been done to him already, Pike thinks—and while unwilling to act or intervene himself, hoping in prayer to continue to waste on, and in doing so somehow change the course of events by wasting—willing at least in thought to take some meaningful action and to live out a more blissful lie—that by continuing blindly forward he might be able to be otherwise—and with his newfound resolve, Pike reaches towards the end table and sips the tea that his neighbor has left for him steeping.

Pike has never been inside the farmhouse before, though he has lived next to it for years—never knew or considered that his neighbor was ever a young girl, or that she had a faceless husband—Pike had always counted on her to be just as isolated and fixed to the despoiled present as himself—not occupying events, but an imagined history waiting to be written—and he supposes that she is gainfully employed, he thinks—based on her morning departures and evening arrivals—that she has a mother and father perhaps, but who is really to say. The neighbor's voice increases in volume, and from the outer room Pike can overhear one side of a conversation—its stops and starts—its laughter with no preface and no context—he wonders to whom she might be talking and toward what end—the Afghan hounds yawning and circling before lying down again—rubbing up against Pike and marking him with their own scent so that they can track him and find themselves again—to be able to find him and tear him greedily apart like Actaeon. His obituary will be brief, Pike thinks— birth and death dates—geography, profession, next of kin—cause of death, *spurned love*—or something more noble—*sepsis via burst appendix*.

Pike reclines on the plush couch. Its embroidered upholstery depicts neat formal gardens in geometric patterns of pastel and metallic thread, with no perspective or depth, in distorted medieval overlay—plan and profile—and smooth to the touch where long silk lines form the reflective pool and rough where the feather stuffing tears violently out of the cushions to prick the skin of Pike's side. He is afraid to sit up, but anxious to remain seated— to accept the neighbor's doubled kindnesses, or to reject her for fear of being ungrateful—which he is, Pike thinks—but he does not want to appear so. Nobody wants your pity, Pike imagines telling her to restore his self-confidence. "What's that," she asks from the next room—and a fear pricks deep within Pike—not knowing whether he had just voiced his thoughts aloud or only in his head—the circling hounds, the surveillance—over the mantle a fall landscape depicts Indiana maples in burnt orange and red. "Oh, good. You're awake," the neighbor says entering the room—and how many times has she come and gone already—how much time has past—Pike's thoughts sounding unfamiliar to himself, as if being mediated through some other source—some hardwood or marble dome amplifying stray syllables with absolute clarity from a great distance, and garbling others closer at hand into distorted echoes that never carry his words directly—mirrored imperfectly like gothic pairs.

Thank you, Pike tries out in his head—attempting not to appear ungrateful—and yet, it feels wrong to hide under his own skin—inside the farmhouse, so familiar—with nothing striking or exceptional about it—handicrafts and a wood-paneled station wagon and the over-the-fireplace television displacing the hearth. Pike is unable to direct his thoughts towards any single point. Hypothesis—the neighbor is conspiring whether knowingly or not toward some malevolent end. Hypothesis—the neighbor was speaking to the hospital charge nurse, laughing and telling jokes at Pike's expense, waiting to be connected to some higher-up to plan said conspiracy—and not even something grand or terrible or with any real tangible gain—but just a random act that accomplishes only itself—that accomplishes nothing—and how can he be a part of what he cannot possibly bear to be a part. The neighbor moves back and forth between the kitchen singing some rhymed children's tune and humming when she does not know the lyrics—it only makes the conspiracy the more plausible—and if coerced, Pike knows now that he would give his neighbor up—a coward at heart who prefers any clear statement even if it is wrong, to risk being wrong, or to celebrate nihilistically that nothing true can ever be said.

Pike calculates probabilities in his head—the likelihood of time that he has left and the relative worth of that time spent held hostage on the neighbor's couch—the odds that they have located him on the grid and that they are converging on his location—how statistics have ruined for him the mystique of all individual achievement. Pike reads the embroidery as an allegory stripped of its referents. Mass produced in some factory, perhaps it never had any referents at all—its laurels and bulls and formal gardens painting processions in their most

raw and immediate forms—to make promises
that they will fail to deliver—and even if they had
they would surely disappoint—the reflective pool,
simply a reflective pool—symbolic of nothing and
reflecting nothing back. The neighbor sits down
across from Pike—he breathes and looks at her
directly. Between them are stacks of unread mag-
azines and unopened mail—envelopes with seemingly familiar handwriting—mail addressed to
him, Pike thinks—mistakenly or deliberately sorted to the wrong address—stolen or forced under—
and how the neighbor is somewhere between the
ages of twenty-five and sixty—with a timeless face
that makes her look both older and younger simultaneously. She does not speak with an accent—she
holds herself with an upright posture—and with
nothing exceptional or suspicious or distinctive at
all—Pike cannot help but assume the worst of her.

The neighbor hums quietly her rhyming tune. It is
the song she sang to her faceless child perhaps, Pike
thinks—and he too is soothed and pacified and
desirous of positing himself as a faceless child—to
curl up on the couch and stay there. In fragments
not much more than a few bars long, she repeats and
gestures toward a whole that is never delivered—
never known or fully remembered—and instead it
lays its assault upon Pike with the false hope that

it can get further next time just by trying harder or gaining momentum. The neighbor speaks in articles and prepositions—the connective tissues between, defining what relationship one should bring to bear, but not toward what to bear it—holding in suspension something as yet unknown—and making Pike inordinately uneasy by all of those who seemingly know precisely what they want—who make firm, active, clear decisions like real adults—building a house, the exact replica of another—caring somewhat, or at all, about the inanely trivial—and what shade of the infinitely many greens they should paint the farmhouse shutters.

When she stops to breathe, the song pauses—and Pike feels a deep sense of suspicion, deception, disregard. He does not wake from his unremembered black, but a sleepwalking clear-sightedness without any sense of his own volition. It takes a moment—Pike feels the textures of the embroidery—reading its allegory, its capitalist sentiment, its misaligned referents and hollow self-definition. Pike sips his tea—still warm—and takes comfort in the fact that he has not lost even more time—not yet been dashed against the thirsty rocks, or held there in perpetuity—and so as not to be confined or become wholly ambivalent, Pikes stands up while he knows he still can. The dogs

sleep soundlessly by the door. Tiny black and orange bugs speckle the crown molding, and Pike
moves toward the foyer with its hardwood som-
nambulant echo—each step and each percussive
beat searching for a rhythm that might draw him
back—the door's carved geometric patterns of circles inscribed within further circles without end.

Pike exits the farmhouse with the sun overhead—
and he hopes that his unremembered self ex-
pressed some gratitude—though not caring or being too selfish to have done so himself. So close to
home—there are many things he does not remember—the faith of having woken up from dreaming
without ever having fallen asleep, the tearing at
himself to get at what is both more and less than
the way things actually are, and how first movers
operate strictly from a void. In what was once a
cornfield, Pike walks into the road lined with sin-
gle-family homes. It sits just off of the main drive
and without an outlet. When an ambulance passes,
Pike knows it is for one of his neighbors or for
himself—and he is cautious in approaching the
bungalow for what might be behind him and what
is surely out front. A car idles several houses down
from his own with two faceless silhouettes inside—a man gardening across from the neighbor's
farmhouse digs his fingers deep into the soil—

and the empty window with its clear line of sight into his living room remains empty—to be home, Pike thinks—scanning the street for the White Fingered Doctor and his bag filled with medicines—or to be alone and isolated with himself, Pike thinks—the one person he cannot truly bear.

Through the black and laurel and bur oak, the sun filters down to cast its sick gray on the pavement. Pike's stretched and foreshortened shadow melts within the overhead leaves that refuse to sit still like water striders on the asphalt. His impulse is to run for the door—to give up the disguise and latch the deadbolt behind him—to be met unceremoniously with a shank in his back—he does not flinch or look over—but facing front like on the parade grounds, he rounds the neighbor's yard and the listless bobbing sunflower heads—his home coming into view in the periphery—only two brick steps separate him from its yellow door. They are watching him, Pike thinks—willful and unwilling—wondering whether to continue walking on the pavement—and without realizing he has already made the choice, Pike quickens his pace—not looking to his right or left, at the men in the idle car, the window or the man gardening—the survivors taken away to the hospital in the ambulance and whoever might be waiting for them—for him—no one and everyone, Pike thinks—to tip them off—Pike moves deliberately.

BOOK TWO

Bloom takes light steps through the doorway and down the stone walk. Stems of grass blur the edges of each square paver and their tiny composite pebbles, sorted by kind, shape, color, size, and spread in packed fields by the hundreds and with the finest machine tolerances to a common burnt red hue. Down at his feet each individual stone—netted with its own spiraling blacks and specks of blue and ferric ochre—anonymous grays of lighter and darker shade and a smooth coarseness to the touch like scraped wax—the daily and repetitive soft oppressions of its scars and pristinely hidden flaws—the straight lines when viewed from a standing height revealing sharp triangular dips and rises when closer—canyons in miniature of each unit atom abutting the next—and the grade and slope of each subsequent arc are pulled like broken compass lines—stretched from dot-to-dot.

His palms spike a dull cutting pleasure at the door—in the hesitation and on-off snap of its internal resistance, the ring of stamped iron—folded and soldered to a point at the peak of its curve—opens to the outside air one of a different kind and color than the one inside of the house—the swirling jarring first steps and acceleration out into the city. He counts backwards from ten to one—concentrating on his breath like he has been told—and passing the hedgerow's translucent greens and shadowed near blacks—over the pavers and the laddered tuffs of lawn—on the far side of the yard a heliotrope traces its unwavering and unrequited love across the sky.

There is nothing like another's faith in you to make you cower, Bloom thinks. In the confidence that Clytie places in him on a daily basis—"Everything is going to be alright," she says—expressions that reveal just how foolish and blind she is to the facts of the matter and to the health of his insides that she does not and cannot see. It is better to treat the opinions of others with suspicion, Bloom thinks—particularly those who think well of you—to reel backwards from any expression of encouragement and fold to any true criticism—to strike the delicate balance between lying and being lied to slant wise—lying to oneself—discursively avoiding the issue at hand and distributing all that needs be done to someone much more capable than oneself and what *should be done* to the ever expanding bank of *things to do*.

He looks back at the Arts and Crafts style farmhouse behind him, the sun shining overhead and each angled shingle resting within the next, the pattern reproduced down the wall to its base where the earth slants away at a lesser slope. It distinguishes itself mostly by its cracks—how those who enter already know how to get lost inside—how what is most familiar is also often the most terrifying—built in the same style and material as other houses on the block, but worn down differently—plagiarized from the same romantic ideal—not in any effort to steal, but to be understood—to steal a little—and every suburban house is a cenotaph to one kind of death or another—to all of the past lives it has held and faithfully let go.

In the driveway, the Lincoln starts with a soft quake. To fear and prepare for the worst, Bloom thinks—contingency plans for failure, divorce, sudden upheaval—mathematical responses of cause and effect—folding in infinite regress back to absolutes where he is always able to count on stasis and paralyzed indulgence. Bloom checks the car's internal gages—clock, radio dial, the upholstery stitching—smudges on the windows painting the roadway in simultaneous haze and clear sunlight—folded and fixed not in time but in their daily looped repetitions. He backs onto the roadway and shifts forward below the overhanging oaks and electrical lines—their crossings and overlaid shadows on the asphalt—the color of the source object mixing with that of the sur-

face upon which it is cast—and with the farmhouse behind him the Lincoln merges out onto
larger and larger streets. It is gauntlet of potential
catastrophe to trust one's health and safe passage
to the collected hands of the masses. In other spe-
cies failed individuals yield lovely symbiotic social groups—or so he has read—bumblebees and
schools of fish—carpenter ants building ornate
excavated basilicas and driftwood patterns out of
decay that only the sea could create otherwise—
though in Indiana that was before the fields of
wind turbines popped up amongst the farms outside of the city—their spinning blades sixty feet
across—to slice with terrible force whatever hap-
less life should enter their paths, Bloom thinks—
just waiting for the right moment to fly off of their
hinges to rip through the doors of his Lincoln.

The traffic light turns red on Keystone Avenue
heading south, and its shaming halogens convict
Bloom of a willful ignorance—or to dream of it—
if only, he thinks—that happiness would come so
easily from without and not always so wretchedly
torqued from within—disloyalty, fraudulence, his
adulterous eyes for the nurse Lola Lola, who he
had met at the city hospital—and in the honey-
combed pattern of the traffic light, all of its tiny
pixilated no's do not simply tell him to stop—it

is resounding—the ordered delivery of their consensus rebuke—red circling patterns with no
descent and no abstaining fill—and all six lanes
of the avenue, three in each direction, are abandoned—waiting for no one—out of habit or failed
pragmatism or imperfect predicting algorithm—
the cross street is open for as far as he can see.

He imagines Clytie moving from room to room
in the farmhouse with purpose. Always in motion
and each action set to a task—not blindly cycling
through sequences of repetitive motion or crippled
by reflex and dead end thoughts played out and
played over—to place him in the exact same position that he was moments before but now with less
time—Bloom knows that he is at his most honest
when enraged by some personal wrong inflicted
upon him—feeling guilty without knowing the
source of his guilt—feeling guilty for so much of
his life that it is difficult to separate the one from
the other—the traffic moves like an accordion
bellows—stretching forward and compressing in
from behind—expansion and contraction—caught
in between those accelerating towards red lights
with those who are coasting—and the Lincoln
turns into a parking garage where it is still dawn
and no longer morning—to breathe the stagnant
exhaust trapped there for days or weeks at a time,

Bloom thinks—exiting the Lincoln and stepping out into the dark and forward onto the city streets.

Outside in the Indianapolis air, the first thing Bloom does is pause and do nothing. To wait and swallow and hesitate—the insurance agents in the business of death and the public utility bureaucrats forming unions—the financial analysts and real estate investors—there is a flatness to their affect—smiling or trying to smile on wide streets with more parking decks than storefronts and towers much like a real city but one that actually exists—playacting as if it were another with stage sets and silkscreened backdrops and a perfectly flat sky overhead without any depth. The businessmen and women walk with self-confidence towards Meridian with an expression of kind placid ambivalence—anonymous and Bloom feels anonymous—not defined by type or name or internal paranoia—but by an inlaid desire to run or to sit very still—to hold himself in stasis and wait for the present to catch up to him or to fall grossly behind.

As the tide of the sidewalk moves east to downtown, Bloom walks in the opposite direction to the canal front and the cement paths that hug its shores—with its equally spaced light posts and romantically clumped trees—the swells of grass

sticking close to the water spill in oblong half circles when given room to rush out from their banks.
In the foreground, two- and three-story triangular
roofs and gables front the rectilinear towers that
rise to form the city's skyline—their horizontal
ribbons and checkered patterns of glass built flush
to limestone. From where Bloom stands he can see
the ninth floor of his own building and his empty office within—the glazing lighting up yellow at
night and reflecting blue during the day—and one
moment he is sitting on the river walk—and just as
quickly—a fall or a fire ignites—dust, munitions,
coal, fertilizer—infectious diseases artfully held behind glass—he puts his best face on—stoic but not
unfeeling—with an empathy gap not maxed out
but in a state of diminished returns, he thinks—an
illegible face of neither happiness nor acute sadness.

The canal connects one arbitrary point in the city
to another; it does not go anywhere. It is not a real
canal with any actual use—but one segmented and
devoid of purpose, destination, will, history—realizing early on that it was far too hard to actually
build and how it is always better to surrender early
than to actually invest. Waiting for the nurse Lola
Lola on a bench, Bloom looks at his watch and down
either side of the walk—late again—his pulse rising, a weakness in his back, thoughts of Clytie—in

the moment he wants to feel pain—not a real pain, Bloom thinks—but the self-indulgent perception of pain, to communicate to others that he is hurting without the actual experience of hurting, or to hurt just enough so that Lola Lola feels guilty knowing that she has done him harm, but not enough to actually experience something substantial or make himself come off as either selfish or spiteful or weak. He pictures himself facedown and floating.

If the she were here, Bloom thinks—he would tell her how he feels—angry without being whiny, wronged not without generosity, empathetic but firm. Not knowing, however, what this would actually look like, he decides on nothing and stares back at the water. On the far shore, figures move along the bank as if cast out of plaster built to a human scale—they are not real, he thinks—sitting around the body of a dead bird talking about how small and frail it is—waving at him and shouting as loudly as they can that such-and-such is *very important*. When time passes, Bloom thinks of Clytie—comfortingly in time—historical—not in the sense of past or future, bodies or loss, but of knowing and being known, of being with, in the connection in between that cannot be defined but allows for definition to take place. With the concrete towers rising vertically off of the hardscape, the apertures at each intersection run as far as the horizon line—figure to ground—positive to negative—in the lattice work of the grid, he is just as easily on as he is off of it—blocked or held up—penitent and apologetic—and the nurse Lola Lola must have been delayed, Bloom thinks— sending him a message in the very form of her absence—an apology for not being there and for any inconvenience that it may have caused him— an extension of her palm and an invitation that she wants him to come to her and not her to him.

*

"Take care," Clytie tells him as he is leaving the house. From the living room—it is a disembodied voice that echoes off of the floorboards and through the opening into the hall—a voice not fully her own, paired in its consistent comforting faith, but one huge and swallowing—forcing him to won- der—whether it is a warning or an order—its am- biguous tone and low sweeping pitch—the gravity implied by the very casualness in which she had said it—sensing in the ineffable that something is there but having no means to reach it—that some- thing is important with no idea what that impor- tance might be—and the sheer meanness of it all to dangle her words in front of his face right as he is going out the door. Bloom refuses to respond. It would only show weakness—as if he were bothered or worried by something unforeseen—as if he were prepared to confess or grovel or apologize. Reaching for his coat and briefcase, the doorknob and its onrush of inflowing air—stepping past the outstretched dogs cooling their bellies on the tile—and without saying a word, he exits the farmhouse and moves over the stone pavers across the yard.

From inside, Clytie watches from the window—Bloom standing next to the Lincoln—his charcoal silhouette on green—a framed shadow draped out into the roadway resting upon the same plane as the telephone lines and overhanging leaves—cutout negatives that are noticeable only by their absence and the echo that hangs long after it is gone. Though with no time to dwell with it, Clytie thinks. She takes her jacket from the coat closet and moves through the side door into the hall—through the kitchen to the garage—chamber upon rectangular chamber—her steps sounding thinner and more metallic on the tile than on the wood—within the concrete resonance chamber—waiting on edge for the sound of his door to slam and for the rev of the Lincoln—the shift and bump of his tires backing down over the curb and all of the internal overlays that she cannot hear—a creature of habit—his breath—a wheezing skipped cadence of short and long—the stretched seat leather and skipping low click of the gear shift.

Clytie is enclosed doubly within. Inside the wagon inside the garage—the temperature cools as she counts backwards from ten before releasing the automatic door and pulling out into the road after him. She can sense it, Clytie thinks—time and time over—the effort it takes to lie to oneself and refuse to place any particular point under pressure—his perfect attentiveness—the curtain pleats—the silence in the room and Bloom's labored short-long inhale and exhale—the insidious burning of their once-history now that it has been called into question, forced into some half-coherence and at the loss of all consistency, if there was any consistency to begin with. They are learning to be more infantile, Clytie thinks—how to do basic tasks—breathe, relax, manage their emotions—to not blindly fire or freeze in steel wax work—dead until I tell you otherwise, Clytie thinks—until she forgets to be angry and is both grateful and disappointed when she finds herself forgetting—again remembering—that she does not in fact believe him.

Clytie tells herself how he is a good man—a minimum compromised despicable good, which of course means nothing, refers to nothing, but for the glossed expectations of what should be. Nothing has gotten us to this point but blind animal begetting, Clytie thinks. A silence hiding between the house cracks—a silence that she used to find such comfort in—one of rest and not of a desperate absence that hangs around each corner unseen—pulses of suspicion and doubt confirmed and disconfirmed with each false negative—each road sound and traffic blinker. The station wagon drifts closer to the Lincoln and Bloom's silhouette becomes visible through the rear window. The will of the traffic moves like a school of fish—easing its constriction just as it tightens—its blind controlled following—and Clytie falls backwards again unconsciously to a safer distance—unable to see or hear—but imagining the space within.

Like all good prejudice Clytie's stems from a latent gap in respect—both outwards and inwards—not so simple as being drawn and pushed away—not afraid of some infiltrating other—of something to lose or any future loss—but pitched by a pining self-scrutiny of the lost-already—of what is real and not imagined—prophecy, the unforeseen—questions that preempt any positive answer and blindly follow the good dead ends of language, seemingly doing their honest blue-collar work, when the outcome has in fact already been in hand for weeks. There is nothing specific that Clytie can point to—Bloom's meek self-suffering posing as truth—the way he sits on the embroidered couch breathing—his dry skin and untrimmed nails—the comforting awful hope that hangs together only so far as it is not looked at too closely—Clytie looks at everything too closely—his skin and what it might have touched and with what pressure—the tail lights of the Lincoln and the matching red glare of the stop light.

The Lincoln drifts over the median line and breaks in upon the dashed yellow animated upon the asphalt. Proof, Clytie thinks—that his mind is elsewhere and that he is not thinking of perjuring himself now—as if it were simply an inconvenient time and that he would gladly perjure himself later—and not thinking about what he failed to witness directly—turning his back and walking away—the silence and the sun overhead at midday—time held still. The outside air courses over the hood of the Lincoln and drops in from behind and is hit again—pockets of greater and lesser pressure folding and absorbing the next car and the next—and Clytie follows in her wagon along the same path through eddies of dust and asphalt and salt.

She does not trust memory but only her ability to predict future events. History does not tell us what will happen next, Clytie thinks—paranoia makes it so—drawn forward slowly by decisions already made and before realizing that there was ever a choice in the first place—to find oneself in the middle of Indiana, on the highway, with no earthly idea how she has come to this place—unable to speak or to call things by name—to test without consequence what has caused this-or-that aphasia or why a white pickup has pulled up beside Bloom and matched the Lincoln's pace. The two cars run in parallel. The windows are black but for the outline of a human shape—intolerant, anonymous—his unconscious drift over the center line now seems even more deliberate—she is sure of it—to get close and to match eyes with the figure in the passenger seat—to share in an instant heat and carelessness and the daily human upkeep of caring for another—decadent meals of sea bream and spigola—and a funeral paid for in advance so as not to trouble their loved ones.

She grips the steering column and follows the tail lights of the Lincoln—a dulled and illuminate red—not focused on her own vehicle, but waiting out the side stitch that burns out of phase with volition—she follows in his wake and mirrors his each turn and acceleration. The way that twice as a child she had escaped gross harm, Clytie thinks—backing into her mother carrying a pot from the burner, she remembers. Clytie knocks into her knees, and the boiling water pours past her shoulders onto the tile—not horribly scalding onto her skin—"By some miracle," her mother had said. The heat pools up on the tile and seeps in through her soles warming Clytie's tiny feet. She remembers running blindfolded through her front lawn—wakeful through the darker and lighter blacks—the burnt earth reds—feeling weightless on the underside of the blindfold. The surface grass shifts to the hard roadway beneath her, and a speeding white pickup swerves to avoid the collision—the pavement gawkers—a rush of air and silence moved to screamed silence. The pickup passes on without stopping—near and imagined—uncertain and unremembered—shifting lanes in and around her.

The two cars turn and turn again as if tied by some invisible umbilical bound to the grid tacking their course through the city. They snake together into the parking deck at ninety-degree angles—one after the other. They park in parallel, and he emerges from the car like a blazon of the body turned over, his back and calves, the vertical lines and his face angled to the ground—so much like her husband but not, Clytie thinks—following the silhouette down the ramp and out into the street. The anonymous are more familiar somehow, Clytie thinks. To expect and anticipate the anonymous—it is stranger to recognize a face than to see a completely new one. Bloom's near recognition is ghostly—wearing the same charcoal suit in which he had left the house this morning—but to know his true identity—he never turns towards her—afraid to see or to be seen—simultaneously wanting and wanting-to-avoid her gaze. He moves with a hitch in his walk that Clytie does not recognize—different in the parking deck, than on the street, than through their marriage together—an upright posture not Bloom's but another's—feeling a pride and a pull towards him that Clytie cannot place of either disgust or attraction.

The man walks as if deep in thought with a stiffness in his shoulders and strain beneath the skin. He charts a course of short straight lines—never true to the path of the sidewalk—but corrected again and again upon another faulty angle—tacking like a sailboat in zigzags away from his office down to the river walk. Time slows and Clytie moves closer—Bloom shielding his face—looking worn upon the bench—taller than he was before—and she wants to seize and to shake him—to commit some gross

hypocrisy she would not stand for herself—to catch
him in the act that she does not want to witness.

Clytie watches him look out over the canal to the
green space and the couples huddled on the op-
posing grass—alone—thankfully alone—to escape
the stress of the office and to learn how to suffer
and give way to oneself—to refuse the urge to re-
align and change course at every errant thought
and accept things as they are—to accept them as
awful, Clytie thinks—hoping blindly that through
chance or self-imposed isolation that they will resolve themselves somehow. Every move he makes
is unconscious, choleric, despicable, blind—his
body held by the bench—the swell of his chest below his suit coat—alive or contingent upon some
higher power—but not thinking about who or
what is behind him—not thinking about what he
is contingent upon—and she feels proud that he
is not meeting someone on the river walk—proud
for what should be taken as given—of floating his
body facedown in the canal south to the Ohio and
West to the Mississippi—if only it went that far.

*

He is taken by the crowd and ushered up the street.
One amidst so many identical others—Bloom can

feel the swell of foot traffic behind him forcing the pace and brushing him to the inside of the walk. Behind his back—irregular waves of hot and cool ambivalence—their independent thoughts and independent purpose—to see him only in silhouette and through the unconscious measuring of his proportions—scale and section—one form against another—and always filtered through the Manichaean and narcissistic sortings of *what applies to me* versus *what doesn't apply to me*—with marked force and efficiency, the former always winning out and reducing him to lists of notable facts—manners, pleasures, propensities for gambling—springboards for all manner of judgment and projection—and pausing, he looks up childlike at the high rise casting over him. In parallel lines built plumb, patterns of receding glass bend and lean out over the sidewalk—the building's vanishing point appears at some impossible distance in lines that seem to separate as opposed to come together—ripped or folded or bent—like an Escher but real—as far as his perception is real—bending—like if just one, amidst the so many thousands on the street were to go missing, he thinks—no one would take any notice.

Bloom had not slept. For insomnia he counts backwards from one thousand down to one with insults and romantic imaginings breaking in upon his meditation—imaginings with Lola—making her wait as he enters the glass doors of the high rise— and imaginings with Clytie—in a garden idyll— winding and spiraling back to thoughts that he is a wretch for such overlap and infidelity of thought space. In his calls to do penance, Bloom plays out in his mind sobering tête-à-têtes with imagined conservative middlemen to receive the goodly sound advice that he is looking for not to think as he is thinking—and yet—conceding the paradox—not knowing now what to believe given that his insides may or may not be lying to him—or lying a little, Bloom thinks—stepping in through the glass doors of the high rise—and at least at the security check, they can see him with some form of clarity.

In the lobby the ambient mechanical and metallic sounds of belts and magnets echo in conversations posing as conversations. Stray words voiced by no one hover in the room and fail to address anyone directly. Through the glass Bloom can see tourists from Wisconsin eyeing him sympathetically and without pretense. He advances in line one unit increment at a time as the x-ray courses god knows what particles through his body— lines in the sand, Bloom thinks—enclosing him from within—inside the high rise, inside the se-

curity check—spheres within spheres—with images of his body projected out onto a monitor
in the adjacent room where they can see his insides and can tell whether or not he is conceal-
ing any metal beneath the surface of his skin.
The Security Guard points to the painted yellow
footprints on the mat and tells him to wait—re-
jecting again and again Bloom's gestures at friendship—what his pulse rate might reveal about his
character—his potential to assume the worst, his
endearing avoidance of all small talk, and less endearing pursuit of all fellowship—to see in vivi-
section down to blood and the tracks of his veins.

Perhaps from the safety of the other side he will
be my friend, Bloom thinks. The Security Guard
is someone to tell secrets to—someone who takes
him seriously—at least more seriously than Bloom
takes himself—as one to do harm—and someone to enliven a will now deadened, because he
cannot seem to be willful himself—to run with
or to run against—down the corridor to the ele-
vators and the offices above, he imagines—as he
stands close by and gathers his keys and wallet and
briefcase—his x-rayed papers transposed to bright
white—washed of all text and contrast—as they
only want to know if he is physically dangerous.
Bloom lingers beside the Security Guard—not

wanting to speak but wanting to be spoken to—
to command himself to express joy without having to be joyous—to be moved without all of the
emotional exhaustion of being moved. "You're all
clear," the Security Guard says—dismissing him
again—the insult of professional courtesy—to
be waved through the line without suspicion—
not even worthy of suspicion, Bloom thinks.

Apart from the time he passes him each morning, there is little telling what the Security Guard
might be doing during the working day—what
cigarettes he may smoke in order to bury god
knows what grandchild—to read everything out
of context—always only a fraction—poems too
quickly—abstracts and tables and labor reports—
irrational and spiritual appetites—never able to
bear witness from birth to death like in gener-
ational novels decades deep, which project far
into the future just to get the faintest sense of
center. Bloom walks down the corridor alone—
waiting for some more convenient time, he supposes—to reconcile with himself with how the
Security Guard did not mean to slight him—out
from under the cameras and without a gun at
his hip—he imagines the Security Guard pat-
ting him on the back approvingly—playing chess
and losing—not wanting to come off as overea-

ger—and the Security Guard would never want
to coerce anyone in the lobby under white lights.

On the floor, Bloom's eyes are brought to constricting point after constricting point. Within the diamond pattern of the marble, burnt red triangular
motifs gesturing forward are met at right angles by
their warm embracing opposites—less-than and
greater-than signs making comparisons and equiv-
alencies—and while never knowing the criteria
being measured, Bloom knows at any given point
where he stands in relation to others—greater than
X and lesser than Y—with the Security Guard behind him and a woman with a canary-yellow bag
and western style string tie out front—walking towards exit and onto the street. The same marble tile
coats the walls and columns and elevator banks.
It hides the building's steel frame and mechanical
conduits—the flywheel governors in the elevator
shafts dangling cages by wires that could so easily
be cut—cleansed and sanitized to a single smooth
surface that reflects light and does not take it in—
to emit slowly the burn of phosphorescence—the
button lights up when pressed and the elevator
chimes as it opens. Bloom pauses and enters. To be
enclosed within—lifted in the cage and accelerated
vertically as the counterweights descend with an
equivalent violence to ease his safe passage above.

I am the happiest of men, Bloom tells himself. He is tired of all the daily animal maintenance—the slights of the Security Guard and the universal neglect—infantile small talk and dogmatic proclamations with nothing in between—to be arbitrarily deified or trotted out to slaughter—the sleepless nights counting backwards with Clytie beside him dreaming peacefully about anyone but him and the elevator dropping in free fall. The two other passengers in the elevator stand upright in a row with their eyes facing the metal doors and their own reflections—their godly provincial conservatism. The man from the Department of the Navy beside Bloom is far too clean-shaven and wide-eyed this morning not to be repressing some horrible childhood torment, Bloom thinks. In order to read his balloon features, he has trouble telling whether the Navy Bureaucrat is on the verge of weeping or of lashing out—spilling confessionally all of his pedestrian thoughts to the Pharmaceutical Rep, frustrated in her own intentions to descend to the parking garage below and trapped in her own novel purgatory going up.

Like all pharmaceutical reps, she holds her impatience just below a fatal stoic social pleasing. Bloom smiles his pursed-lipped smile, searching for something to say—something normal and true and interesting, Bloom thinks—with an ethic of casual disregard to whatever the response might be in order to set everyone at ease. The display in the elevator counts the floors as they move vertically up the building—with an increase in energy and increase in the level of threat, Bloom thinks—the Navy Bureaucrat breathes in shorter and shorter breaths, and the Pharmaceutical Rep smiles back at Bloom with slant eyes filled with suspicion—never to actually say good morning or to volunteer whatever national or personal crisis is pending—or even to offer up their names, Bloom thinks—and not even their real names, but just ones to fit the moment and to serve their deviled turn.

Shifting his weight onto his opposite foot, the Navy Bureaucrat must be thinking of childhood humiliation, Bloom thinks. The Pharmaceutical Rep continues to hold her smile—now looking at no one and comforting only herself—lying that she is happy inside and selfishly turning inward—crossing another set of floors and another—and now it is really too late to talk about their childhoods, Bloom thinks—their fathers, assuming they have fathers, and the difference between feeling and affect—acute and abstract pain—Clytie back home in their Arts and Crafts style farmhouse and how

disturbed her thoughts and paintings have become—black and white isonometics of the body as
if she were drawing city streets, he thinks—yellow
and blue pencil lines of the farmhouse rendered
in overlaid plan and perspective—*abstract*, Clytie
calls it—but Bloom knows it for the nonsense it
really is—impossible to view anything in more
than one dimension at any one time—to skirtingly
switch between faces and candlesticks—the Pharmaceutical Rep's smile and the Navy Bureaucrat's
fidgeting—pressed by some vainglorious tempta-
tion to smile or fidget all of the time—or to simply give way and to have the impression vanish.

*

Bloom has grown taller. She is sure of it—no longer five foot nine inches as he left the house this
morning, but six feet and growing—his hair shorter and a darker shade of black—with slimming
straight lines more universal and more threatening—that if she could smell him, she would be
embathed in the rosemary pomanders that mask
plague and death—speeding the spread of disease
by encouraging her to breathe in more deeply—
the spice and resin and whatever will serve for the
present purpose to hide what's underneath. Clytie
measures him for a second time using her thumb

for a reference—the proportion of his raised fore-
arm to the height of his navel—the length of his
elongated palm and stretched forefingers—one
hand gripping his briefcase and the other spiraling
in upon itself into a tightly shelled fist. The har-
monics of his body sing in shrill atonal pulses—
exhales of steam and shifts of internal pressure—
the ambulance siren carrying yet another virgin
passenger—and the cadence of his heart beating at an uneven 3/3 and not balanced 4/4 time.

From where Clytie stands behind him she cannot see his reactions to those gathered on the far
side of the canal. In the sun and pocketed shade
they spread like gas molecules in twos and threes
evenly over the bank—red on the lawn's green—a
woman with a bonnet focuses in upon her hands
and the man smoking beside her looks plaintively
forward across the water. A child wearing a white
dress meets the eyes of a woman sitting on the
grass with her own child—and the first's mother
looks the other way—askance or down—soldiers
and trumpet sounds—canes, umbrellas, bouquets
of flowers—another pair and another—meeting or
failing to meet each other's eyes. In the flatly se-
rene, dozens of periscopic lines of sight spike their
frightened, internal, scalene oscillations—if she
could only map it, Clytie thinks—and for a mo-

ment she needs to look away—back at Bloom sitting upon the bench—unmoved and ambivalent—or not close enough to see the tiny beads of sweat on his neck or to hear his frightened calls for light.

Clytie does not put much stock in the natural world. Her paper skin is dry though the humidity is heavy—and she is unable, she thinks, to take even a step without crushing whole colonies of life—moth or box elder bug flailing their stick legs on their backs—wishing she could get around to the other side of him somehow to confirm his identity and trace his reactions to the placid faces on the river walk—to enlist some co-conspirator to watch from a different angle to share in her internal distortions. Scanning the opposite bank Clytie looks at each erred figure in the eye—one at a time, in judgment not without sympathy—the child, the woman, the soldiers in uniform—the ineffable alignments and pulses that she is not even sure are possible for another to see.

They are deadened, Clytie thinks—sitting contentedly on the canal bank—picnicking and at rest—not wanting to look at their husbands or wives and invent false histories no more untrue than the one's they tell themselves and each other—the smell of sassafras—in order to discover

new worlds and new diseases—frauds and hypocrites and convicting Herods—only the child in
the white dress is benevolent, Clytie thinks—and
if only the child were ten years older, she would
enlist the child to be her co-conspirator—to
share her views from the opposite shore—and
never look at Bloom directly so as to call attention to yourself, Clytie advises—but from the
side unseen—to report back whether or not he
reacts or burns blue candles to signal his arrival.

She pictures Bloom leaning on a parapet. The city
blurred before him in hatched grays—the skyline
is undefined beyond its outline and evidence of a
shaping hand—his core is solid black with softer
edges—leaning his elbows upon the rail—Clytie
can see through him, she thinks—floating where
his feet should touch the ground—to tip forward
or back—*Emilia Galotti* resting on his nightstand.
Twice as an adult she had escaped gross harm, she
remembers—in Indianapolis driving her station
wagon at night with sand and oil like blinding
burst capillaries on her windshield—the oncom-
ing light reflected and refracted in all directions
but forward—magnified so that she sees only
black and blinding white—shadowed promises
of roadway—Clytie turns up the off-ramp not
knowing that the traffic is coming from the op-

posite direction. Once, years later, she had been called *dangerous*. Looking down four stories from the balcony flat—it is sort of an in between height, Clytie remembers thinking—wondering whether or not the fall would do it, or whether jumping would simply cause some foolish break and only serve to confirm their judgment in the first place.

She is not deceiving herself, Clytie thinks—rising from the bench he reaches an even greater height—his proportions stretched to fill the full plane of her vision. Walking back the way that he came, Clytie follows cautiously leaving plenty of distance between them—close enough to see but not close enough to hear his confession—and unable to forgive what she has not heard directly. At each stoplight, the cars pack together in neat lines before they are released up the avenue and stopped again—stacked in longer and longer arresting clumps—valves not circulating blood—but right-angled crossings that slice any common work and common fellowship. Bloom's stride is punctuated by quick steps and slow languorous pauses—looking down or up, but never at the faces of the other pedestrians on the street—not thinking about the silence that fell between them as he left the house this morning or the time they both felt the same shudder in the earth disconfirmed by everyone else they asked—to hold against him what she knows she could not possibly expect—and yet Clytie feels it anyway and scolds herself for feeling it.

He stops and flexes his neck on the sidewalk—joint, ligament, constricting or expanding muscle—skin and pocketed pores hiding below the surface all of the stringed mass and fibers and liquid gelatins that would refuse to hold their shape without it— slowly dying—his fingernails continuing to grow. Clytie waits on a square of cement that he had just passed through the moment before—feeling the current of his wake still coursing through space, as if she were sitting on a train—always from *nowhere to nowhere*, watching the cars on the adjacent track pull out and feeling the stationary force pushing Clytie backwards—certain that she is moving when she is standing still—the internal tide of Bloom's once-presence—of past and future memories that she is certain he is not thinking about.

At her funeral, they will bury her between trees so that her neighbors can enjoy the buffer of roots between them, Clytie imagines. The child in the white dress will only understand years later— Bloom shaking hands with guests and setting out flowers and rosemary perfumes to seal her body in a cloud—fending off and inviting in—how this is a boundary to be crossed passively and unseen—to breathe in the masking vapors that they can sense and the airborne spores and particles that they cannot—those that will cure any illness and those that will make them sick if they breathe in too deeply.

The contraction of disease often goes unnoticed—perhaps it has happened already, Clytie thinks—a fault or fracture—consumption sparked at the very moment that Bloom tells some off-color joke or says nothing at all—not that it is his fault, but the timing couldn't help—heartlessly carrying on as if we all weren't spiraling toward death anyway, Clytie thinks—and as if death were a secret that could be avoided indefinitely just by failing to acknowledge that she is not as actively dying as she otherwise might be. They laugh in the kitchen, and the girl in the white dress lights a scented candle that fills the air with oils—striving to hide the smell of decay and unwashed hands—blips of replicating DNA steering their lives hard to the left or right—and Bloom, refusing to turn around, stares blankly up to the sky. He raises his arm above his head to blot out the sun as if willing an absence—anything but to careen sideways—and never to notice or to acknowledge when they already have.

The custom is to hold out for recovery, Clytie thinks. Standing behind the crowd as he enters the building, Clytie looks through the glass curtain wall and watches him advance through the security line—one after another—wools and cottons and flammable synthetics—surely they will see him for who he really is, Clytie thinks—standing close to the Security Guard and lingering there— wondering what they can possibly be waiting for and why the Security Guard doesn't grab Bloom by the lapels and throw him to the tile—to inject him with some sedative or anoint him with some healing salve. Perhaps the Security Guard is playing possum, she thinks—to hold out hope—but they wave Bloom forward and he passes through unadulterated. Clytie watches him recede down the hall—further and further—and by some trick of the eye, maintaining his height—as if refusing to fold down the picture plane—as if fulfilling a prophecy for she does not know yet what.

*

Bloom exits on the ninth floor and moves over the threshold, the thin line of negative light between carpet and elevator bottom, and he enters the office as if drawn by some perverse gravity feeling the shift in air pressure over the gap. The floor is divided into mathematical grids—cubicle banks nested within rows of columns—offices along the outer walls and the conference rooms on axis with the elevator doors—to look down upon the framed views of Indianapolis—the War Memorial and Benjamin Harrison House—the City Hospital and its ambulance bay and the continual dropping off and retrieval of patients—those who are dying and those who have already passed—those shuttling back and forth between home and hospital and back again. "They're waiting for you," the Receptionist says—as if to a child with no hope for an aimful life, Bloom thinks—afraid of being treated with consideration and guilty at the first note of compassion—appreciative in the abstract of the Receptionist's gestures of kindness, but kindnesses, he thinks, that are not at all valued or wanted.

In his office, he feels on display behind the partitioned glass—primed for zoological study or psychological testing before any agreed upon code of ethics—learning to be afraid of himself—to react to particular sounds and smells and shades of blue with horror or lust—engrained reactions and reflexes that he does not understand and cannot trace the roots of their origin. He dials the hospital and leaves a message with the Charge Nurse. Within the panopticon—a prisoner viewed from all angles—the Charge Nurse's dismissive tone inflames to self-righteousness—continually inhaling her *odors of sanctity*, Bloom thinks—to have no importance of her own but vicariously sticking close to those who do when they are dying. "I'll tell her you called," the Charge Nurse says—knowing that she won't—knowing that any human connection is too much for the Charge Nurse—that she hates him, Bloom thinks—or views him with an indifference worse than hate—insignificant, disposable—feeding the nurse Lola truths that imply more than their face value and not the falsehoods she prefers. She doesn't want honesty, Bloom thinks—but to be lied to softly so as to be able to believe in anything at all, to get the best out of herself by stooping below one's own self-respect, and condescendingly believing the lies that he tells her.

At his desk Bloom angles himself away from the interior cubicle bank with his back to the reception desk—it is the only position in his office where it is difficult to tell whether he is looking down at his work or absently out the widow to the street below—tiny automobiles coursing up and down Meridian—and through the glass inside the adjacent offices, he can see others mirroring his same gaze—a firing squad or ambush tracing one individual after another—recording what doors they enter and the timing and pace of their travel—what history of feeling sits behind their inscrutable faces—and what precisely it is like to keep their own dissimulations to themselves.

His nerves sit on the edge of solidity and emotional cracking. It is equally as rational, he thinks, to spontaneously burst into tears as it is to stoically bear them—and at any moment, it could go either way—the hollow in his throat and pressure in the liver—bile and odd mixtures of choler and out-of-balance humors forming oblong human-like bodies devoid of any action or agency—lying dormant, Bloom thinks—the patch of dried skin on his hand spreads as he scratches. The Receptionist enters again and leaves a stack of papers on his desk— *Apage Santana*, he thinks—having to guard his soul against the infiltrating other—and to deflect their demands for his presence in the conference room like a Marine's call to attention. They are not interested in his thoughts or actions, but merely want for him to be present, Bloom thinks—to sit idly dead in his chair—where his central task is to not disturb the Townsman in his unwavering and unapologetic calls for patriotism and capital—unmoved and uninterested in anything anyone else might say—but confused to stoppage by any active rebellion, erasure, any out of place furniture in the room—and where his own ability to satisfy others' needs rests solely in his active non-presence.

Bloom can only imagine what must be happening in the conference room. The Union Official hesitating and decrying his place in the world—hyperbole, scapegoat, broad milk-white abstractions—with the blank-faced Townsman across from him at the table jotting his observations down in ink—ceaselessly writing when there is no need yet to be writing—at least until the Union Official signs—and yet the Townsman is relentless—hand to paper—transcribing his affirming notes to himself and disparaging commentary on others—recording and dissecting everyone's movements and actions—the Union Official's flattened bovine face—his dead eyes, the same color as the background—and Bloom's transparent mistrust and crisis of faith—each breath and pause and innocuous remark—to be seen in all of one's waste and minutia—or worse—to be seen specifically by the Townsman and to be recorded in his ledger for god knows what purpose.

Bloom closes the glass door behind him and tries listing his anxieties—that at base there is only stasis, that Clytie no longer loves him, that he made a fool of himself in front of the Security Guard by lingering too long, and that the labor dispute will go on in perpetuity—failure, isolation, chronic fatigue, an incapacity to handle even basic responsibilities, the past, the aged, large densities of like-thinking youth—how the Townsman is most certainly counting the seconds on his wristwatch waiting for him to arrive and planning some vengeful response regardless of whether he does or he does not—with no means to escape—documenting all of Bloom's movements, actions, and internal thoughts that he should not have access to but somehow does—unfettered access to his insides, Bloom thinks—Clytie, Lola, his thoughts on the Townsman—doubly and triply reflected—to know that the Townsman knows that he knows, Bloom thinks—and he counts backwards from ten to calm himself and looks out of his window down to the street bottom.

Walking north along Meridian a woman takes nineteen seconds to travel between light posts. Her is posture upright—her respiratory rate normal—having no trouble this morning making basic decisions and at peace with her own mortality, Bloom thinks—and on her way to visit friends—the misanthrope with scores of friends. Some nineteen seconds behind her, another woman follows her same path—stopping when the woman stops—accelerating when she accelerates—mirroring her speed and posture and ambivalent air. Bloom stands to get a better angle—straining against the plane of the glass as the figures cut perpendicularly across the side of the building—slowly cutting off his view—pressing his hands and face hard against the window as if he is able to rotate the whole building from inside.

From the ninth floor they appear tiny along the street—colored specks and atoms—a field of blue and punctuated yellow and a flatness promising depth that Bloom doubts is actually present. Above—the blackened windows in the adjacent buildings are filled with spectators that Bloom cannot see—looking down at the women with suspicion and back at Bloom in his own exposed looking—wondering whether the second figure is poised to strike or whether she is simply walking in the same direction as the first—though from a distance, a strike isn't real anyway, Bloom reminds himself—but flattened to silence and the smell of masked perfumes—through glass there is nothing but the picture plane—no scream, no affecting terror—but marked color and placid faces perfectly content.

It is a sickness simple enough to diagnose. To those who are on the edge and vulnerable, every-

thing is prophetic—the symptoms of acute fear—
fever, high blood pressure, night sweats, muscle
tremors—expressions of abrupt kindness and an
unflappably calm tone of voice—tea leaves fore-
telling death and a history of enraged outbursts—
and tracing the trend line backwards, signs of what
the future will bring, Bloom thinks—for Clytie,
himself, the woman stalking the other across the
city moving outside the frame of his window. Her
bag is filled with poisons, Bloom imagines—she
speaks softly and gestures out with a smile—
not like a real villain—unaware that she is playing a part in something much larger than herself—something fated—as if the awnings above
the street café are poised fall and crush everyone
underneath them—as if she were to place a mirrored sheet of glass below the other's mouth in
order to tell if the first woman is still breathing.

*

It is not unreasonable to follow, Clytie thinks—
if the Security Guard refuses to see him for who
he really is and the authorities fail to react—if
he should refuse to turn and face her squarely in
the eyes. Everything is framed as a problem to be
solved and not the awful inevitabilities they actually are to be resignedly accepted. The overhead

lamps cast their light down to the marble floor and reflect back upon the underside of his palms whatever defensive scars he has hidden there. Through the window glass she watches him walk to the back of the lobby. In cutout planes, the images stack and layer—the backs of the sidewalk pedestrians with the reflection of their faces upon the glass. The security check inside is smudged with water stains like cataracts or the suspended grains of light that signal a seizure in the moment just before losing consciousness. There are others in the lobby who seem unaware of the danger that they are in, and Clytie wonders what improvised violence he will level on those waiting beside him—waiting for the elevator—waiting to be trapped inside with a villain who acts upon whatever malevolent instinct or failure of will is inside of him—Bloom enters the cage and disappears up the spine of the building.

She traces his travel up along the high rise's exterior. Polished limestone squares of white on off-white—broken by metal lines and the patched reflections of the opposite building like memory cards of some childhood familiarity—something she has seen before but is unable to identify in its context—to see the whole from the fractal part—layers of solid and void in their full range of imperfection in story after stacked story. If she were

to paint the scene, the verticals would fold inwards
and vanish deep within the canvas, Clytie thinks—
at narrow angles, she can see the fractions of discol-
ored ceiling titles within the offices overhead—the
mirrored outlines of spectators looking down upon
her with suspicion—and inside the elevator Bloom
is poised to strike—never to believe that he would
be capable of such violence—the overhead display
counting the numbered floors as the elevator ascends—Clyting silently counting backwards in
her mind in order to calm herself—the traffic and
pedestrian white—slowing and accelerating—and
when the present breaks in upon her, she can no
longer see what is happening inside the cage—the
measurable and the immeasurable—what she can
only imagine or refuse to recognize—Bloom stepping off on the ninth floor and entering his office.

Perhaps her memory is faulty and he was planning
to leave all along. Perhaps he had caught a glimpse
of her following and is now drawing her in close to
be trapped inside. Forcing herself forward, Clytie
passes a woman with a canary-yellow bag rushing
in the opposite direction—pulling Clytie's attention to follow with her eyes as the woman walks
down Meridian away from her—Clytie's thoughts
feeling material somehow—as if they are visible to
those watching from above—feeling the force of

expectation and readings known and unknown—
and what invisible pricks are caught and adopted,
recognized and ignored, and what other simulta-
neities are just as real as the present. But turning
again—Clytie directs her gaze away and follows
Bloom inside the lobby and its still unnatural air.

She has suspected him for weeks now. Rewriting
the past, the present, the smell of each carnation
blossom, days when she was perfectly trusting un-
wind every time her will goes slack. It is a faith held
fast by desire and not point of fact. Wanting to believe without actually believing, Clytie torques herself in the shape of one who does in the hope that
mere desire will make it so. She feels his judgment
just below the surface. Her mind speeding lateral-
ly—how no one cares about her childhood unique-
ness or crook-necked synaptic jumps—the images
behind her eyes of black cubes are thrown down to
the ground and fracture into flat planes—playing
out their lives within the composite rubble—it is
an illusion and not a hallucination because it stems
from an actual image—a phantom pain and weakness in her back—divination, crystallomancy, Vir-
gilian lottery—by whatever means necessary—no
longer trying to foretell the future, but to find any
sense of solidity she can in an ever-fracturing present that keeps shifting and countering like a boxer.

Clytie moves through the security line and surrenders her skin to the x-ray. Millions of high energy waves are thrown through her body—deflected and reflected—in order to see you for who you really are, Clytie thinks—bone and cartilage and the absence of firearms—repressed neo-puritans who never really work especially hard but want others to think that they do—black sheep hypocrites with the same tastes as their pre-literate children. She walks slowly through the line pained with a keen awareness of the absences on either side of her—pockets of air and space where someone could be standing, Clytie thinks—where they could be holding her hand and telling her the history of the city, themselves, their frightening near collapses and full on implosions. The overhead lights are unwavering, she notes—providing neither shade nor shadow nor break in intensity—the overexposed bright white of a flash bulb that reveals everything—which is to say nothing—and in the deadened heat of the lobby, everyone can see right through you.

*

The Receptionist enters Bloom's office saying nothing—the door and window glass—skin, bone, air, blood—the indiscriminate crossings and tear-

ing apart of any illusion at privacy—the boundary between himself and others is a porous line.
When the Receptionist finally says nothing at all,
Bloom knows that it is time to carry out the mo-
tions of being an entrenched human being—to
supplicate himself to the Townsman, or the Union
Official, or whomever should need to be suppli-
cated to—to put on his egalitarian and apathetic
face—and speak in a language of silence and re-
fusals built up from years of working together and
not speaking. He is unable to let go of the sinking
thought that the more he resists the tighter and
harder they will finger his rib bones—wishing that
he could locate the source of such proddings so
that he might befriend them and convince them
to stop—convince them that their delusions ar-
en't any more real than his own and that their
soft repressions are just as juvenile and just as
crippling. The receptionist stares—there is movement on the other side of the wall—and there is
little point now, Bloom thinks—in trying to win
over those who have already turned against him.

He turns away from the Receptionist and walks
out of the office—through the field of columns
and cubicles—passing one square and one unit after another. Bloom measures time using two dis-
crete systems. In the first, the twenty four hours to

the day are painfully subtracted—by minute and
by second—counting down in their pessimistic
death march each lost, despairing, failed opportunity to do something useful—whatever that might
mean, Bloom thinks—but never doing it—or never enough—each passing moment only confirming his own continued purposelessness. Time two,
rather, counts forward from any number of personal emotional fits—the time since leaving the farmhouse, the time since calling the Charge Nurse, the
last moment he felt tethered and connected—and
between them whole days are lost—Bloom slips
outside of any objective measurement, and only
after the fact is he able to chart his own solipsistic,
$T2$, onto the wider regressive, $T1$—the Julian to the
Gregorian—the Week of Three Thursdays—unable
anymore to make the conversion between them.

He is late—the conference room is coated in wood
panels and notched cornice lines—built-in decorative half-columns with no structural significance
at all are offset from the grid and are broken only
by the metallic diamond patterned wallpaper that
reflects the overhead light. In the Midwest, the
tasteless compensate for their folksily garish pec-
cadillos by buying more expensive folksiness—and
the Townsman fails to look up as Bloom enters but
makes a note on his legal pad—something about

war, Bloom supposes—something important and with bravado—not the documentation of his presence, attendance, the continuation of his life, such as it is—his heart still beating—but recording something striving, Bloom thinks—something natural.

The two parties pass papers back and forth across the table without speaking. With the Union Official on one end and the Townsman on the other, they cross out lines in the contract in red and write their respective additions, amendments, and parentheticals in black—abusive or constructive commentary directly to one another in blue—circling and re-circling until they both initial the bottom of the page and pass the sheet to the secretary who makes live corrections in his computer, only to be printed out anew and sent through the cycle again. The pages of the contract are out of order—some moving back and forth four times between them—some six—some ten. They call and re-call previously agreed upon sheets back into the circle. They breathe like asthmatic dogs and read with unnatural speed. The Union Official's eyes, seemingly unable to move horizontally, but scan up and down the page consuming whole lines in a single moment—emptying them of all sound and internal harmony—summed and diluted to their simultaneous maximum—and a particularly trenchant page, *Number Five*, has to be re-entered in its original state after being passed and re-passed without agreement until it is entirely blackened in illegible red and blue swirls.

The two parties work without pausing—passing papers with their right hands to the piles on the other's left—the stack in front of one rises and then the one in front of the other. Bloom can hear the air conditioning and paper scratches, the faint traffic burn from nine stories below trapped and muted between the panes of glass—enflamed pileups and muzzled screams—the inescapable anechoic blood flow that rests below silence. Bloom pretends to read through proofed sheets like a slave testing the food of a king for poison— and on points where the parties cannot come to any agreement, they roll dice. The Townsman opening up the contract turns to the line and page thrown by the Union Official's roll—"In the event of a natural disaster," he reads—and it is a positive outcome for the Townsman, given the even number of syllables in the line—though the roll was odd—and the Union Official believes just the opposite—that Americans, particularly patriotic Midwesterners, lacking any sense of irony, treat things so very literally that in Indianapolis *natural disaster* means *natural disas-*

ter no matter how many times they throw lots and exercise their opportunities to reconsider.

How many times could it have been otherwise, Bloom thinks—to not be wearing his neat twill charcoal suit or taking his and Clytie's weekly trips to the movies, the inexpensive dinners out, or long minutes staring off at himself that provide the impression of thoughtfulness—but rather—a crash or sudden engine failure—inexplicable mechanical sounds that amount to something rather than nothing—all of the would-be hitchhikers that he had considered but failed to pick up—all those who would have done him some irreparable harm, Bloom thinks—a nicked scratch to the neck or Ondine's curse forcing him again and again to remember to breathe.

It is really a two-step process, Bloom thinks. One—develop violently distorted views, particularly those with regards to the confidence one holds in oneself. Two—express these views with confidence, never questioning either one's self-imposed distortions, which with time will become rote, or the potential for self-change, which is now unnecessary. At the same time, ignore all other inputs both from one's critics and one's supporters. It is not a god complex per se, Bloom tells himself. In such cases, one defers to an image of themselves, *self-as-god*, to do all of the common good works of one's true self, *self-prime*, in the here-and-now. Or in other words, while one strives to be god, they are always in fact crippled by their own earthly self-loathing they are not.

*

Clytie is taken by the paintings on the lobby floor—ink blots and lines over rectangular fields of primary colors—so pleasing in their lack of coherence, their verisimilitude, their static indifference to pain and active resistance to joy—a refusal to bleed for any abstract everyman and to forget all particularity for the sake of nothingness—in Rorschach blots that signal death or fertility—definitions may call things into being but willfully refuse to tell Clytie what she is to do next. The pessimists are always technically more correct, she thinks—death is unavoidable—the earth will at some point fuel some exploding star—ours or another's—Bloom will leave, and the smell of gardenias will ferment to putrid decay—and so on and so forth until collapse—unfortunately siding with them commits her to despair and avoiding them fully turns her shallowly inwards.

The lobby is still. The Security Guard paces along the far side of the hall, holding himself within his chronic hysteria, apathy, mania, abulia—epileptic spurs and inert deadweights that paralyze him into *toeing the line* no matter how pointless or arbitrary that line might be—defending the lobby like Verdun and holding on to what is lost already. The Security Guard's hands are unfit for fight or flight, Clytie thinks. The skin on his knuckles is smooth like an oyster's, and his skeleton fingers bounce off of his thumbs in sequence. The rhythm is irregular, but it is not without logic—tapping out S-O-S in Morse code—jazz improvisations that go unrecorded—large portions of himself drop to the marble floor in the form of dust or skin cells left there to decay—sucked into the air vents and blown outside of the building—washed and sanitized and inhaled by Clytie on the other side of the room possessed by some controlling medium to hold herself still.

The Security Guard's silhouette folds into the checker-patterned backdrop on the wall—the hairs on his arms—the lines in the tile—the lips and lids of his eyes. His head droops toward the floor and alternates between contemplating one form of despair and another, Clytie thinks—waiting for the next thing not to happen—for the sound of one echo to follow upon the next—step after step—spike and distortion—everything in perfect symmetry—inkblot to color field to the painting's frame on the wall—the scale magnifies, but at each level it is the same. *Bloom* is to *Fidelity* as *Good Taste* is to *Abject Bitterness*, Clytie thinks. *The Security Guard* is to *Marriage* as *Taking Out One's Rage Onto Strangers* is to *Preserving the Illusion of Peace on the Home Front*. The echo in the lobby crescendos, but the sound lags in delay as if the air has changed and the sound waves travel at a lesser pace—a lower pitch—to fail in their attempts to pierce the walls and reach the steel frame within—to crawl up through the skeleton of the building and be conducted along the metal beams to the offices above.

In their life together the Security Guard would never leave his perfect wife for her, Clytie imagines. Though if he did, she could not respect him anyway—the lying adulterer that he is—and the sun that casts through the entry glass angles upon the western wall and cuts rectangles of light onto the marble—square upon square—the ambient and even coat of the overhead bulbs attempting to wash the sun from its backdrop. As the elevator opens, this same light pours inside uninvited before Clytie can suggest that it might want to stay behind on this trip—before she even has the chance to think of it—the resounding mechanical echo shifts inside the elevator shaft. As one thought in her mind calls itself forward, the internal chorus flows and follows in a torrent after it—impulse and opposite—in every mirrored reflection—Clytie's thoughts churn like a gospel song reinforced and undercut with each new repetition.

The doors close, and her reflection pans into view. Staring back at her own gaze—it is not the face that she remembers, Clytie thinks—but thinner, softer, with kind obtuse angles to her cheekbones that spill subtly forward—not hers but another's—the reflection wears tight black cotton slacks and a matching black crewneck as if she is a stage hand for the community theater's production of *Who's Afraid of Virginia Woolf* with its timid, fearful, weak-kneed leads who fail to project their own voices—her sickly copper-toned skin on the metallic door masks a disease haloed in bridal crowns—compensating for something she does not believe in the first place—that even in taking on its greater sense of gravity—the inside mirror will carry the same lie that she repeats to herself outside of its reflection—that it was this way all along since the beginning.

Clytie imagines standing outside the farmhouse at dusk. The unlit windows are darker than the sky, and those enlivened within shine into the half-light. She can see the side of a dressing table cut off from view by the edge of one window—a lamp framed—a backlit curtain—Bloom's silhouette with his face held in shadow shouting out to no one in particular how much they are in love, and the banded trees in the background freezing in the wind like flowstone. The path below them leads into black under the canopy, swallowing up the dark, and the blues and grays of the sky threaten either to move forward toward her or harmlessly off to the side— in disbelief that this same wind would possibly take the storm away—she is alone in the elevator. If only someone were there to listen to how she cannot accept Bloom's offer of a blessed life, and how she would gladly gamble away what is already counterfeit. Her throat constricts. Her hands tighten into compact fists. In the reflection upon the door, Clytie can see her hair and nails grow into live viny threads and sharpen to points—extending before her in the reflection. She looks down at her hands—the underside of her palms—as the elevator starts with a jolt, it ascends vertically up the building, counting the floors it passes with its red illuminate lights.

*

In order to foretell the future Bloom rolls dice like the Union Official and reads the corresponding line on the page of the contract he is holding. *Always keep your own self-interest at heart in order to excuse fault and take credit where none is due*, Bloom tells himself. *Submit quickly and without question to self-pity as it will always take the side of one's Id*, he tries again. A more optimistic person would respond with excitement and possibility—feigning abstractions unspoiled from actually living and being alone—of having his every move and breath dissected by the Townsman and cursing to himself on his drive in the Lincoln—his palms punching the steering column as the red lights stare back at him as he idles—the smell of exhaust and the drone of the road sounds—waves and Doppler swells and the scratching of pens on paper—Bloom concentrates on the pain in his bruised palms—the damage to the wheel. He did not want to do any real harm, Bloom thinks—to break or curse or bend from how he imagines himself to be—to call things by their real names and for what they actually are—to be flooded by a feeling that cannot be parsed into neat categories and deliberate courses of action—but in spite of himself, or perhaps quintessentially so—pathetically and pragmatically wanting to be *futile*.

He stacks papers in the conference room in silence. The men beside him work diligently—upbeat and smiling. The Union Official asks with interest about Clytie, his weekend, his unfulfilled childhood aspirations—to avoid situations such as this, Bloom thinks—to avoid being dragged across some urban moor to marry the devil. Bloom holds his posture upright—his eyes scan the Union Official and the Townsman for some shared hardship—dropsy, rickets, diseases as yet unknown and without a name—it must even out somehow—not wishing them real harm and not wanting them to suffer, not wanting to throw the switch in the tracks and bear witness to its bloody effects—to plaintively and obsequiously walk away from the accident—but silently and spite-fully wishing that they would feel some chronic ache or loss, some continual nagging itch below their skin, just to make things a bit more fair.

Bloom's pulse accelerates. He sweats in his wool suit. Whatever fixed number of heartbeats he has been allotted in life, they are methodically sub-tracted and frittered away, he thinks—pretend-ing to read the freshly printed edits, commentary, composite summaries—Bloom watches the black lettering on the page grow in vegetal patterns out from its endpoints—like the diamond motifs on the inner walls or a möbius strip of black cycling in upon itself—the extension of each vectored line spreading to the edges of the page—winding and crossing—the next letter and the next—expanding over the white and intersecting through the adjacent letter in ornate arabesque designs. Bloom tries to forget the fact that it must be an illusion and not a hallucination because the source is real, if ever distorted, and perhaps they will be my friends in the end, Bloom thinks.

In the purgatory of the office, they pick at Bloom's exposed consciousness. The Townsman records each word that he says and doesn't say—each action that he preforms and fails to preform, and every gray-matter twitch and physical thought—Bloom's tendons flexing below a translucent skin—the building up and mostly breaking down of muscle through the slow atrophy of age and disuse. The Townsman notes the particular shade of blue of his deoxygenated blood—violently attempting to transpose life and feeling unwillingly onto paper. The room swells and the city turns in on itself. He has never been fit for the city, Bloom thinks—not even a real city—London with its stabbings and Chicago with its profound compensating good will—Indianapolis with more war memorials and fewer battlefields than any other in the country. The receptionist gestures toward him from the open door as if holding a knot in her throat. "A call, Mr. Bloom," she says.

By the time he reaches his office, Lola has already hung up, or who he assumes is Lola. Bloom holds the receiver to his ear and listens to the electric howler tone that screams in shrieking indifference that the other line is off of the hook—Lola Lola having impatiently dropped the receiver in furstation, he imagines—some noxious patient down the hall from her in the hospital willfully coding just to spite him—drawing her attention away—and Bloom is afraid of what that symbolically might mean. It is not dissimilar to celebrating his birthday, Bloom thinks—May 4, 1970—and how Clytie tries to advise him every year to "Try not to think about it." He tries not to think about it—fails. Tries not to listen to the electric pulse of the dial tone before hanging up the receiver.

Perhaps he simply wasn't fast enough, Bloom thinks—and what separates his potential happiness from a metaphorical knife in the back is roughly thirty-five seconds, give or take. In the pause he took before rising from his chair—his restrained steps and measured breathes walking back to his office and through the open door—never wanting to appear overeager—never wanting to appear in front of the Townsman as anything but *meeting obligations*, Bloom thinks—to work and appear pleased and to never feel joy—goodly puritan and puritanical—learning to sleep soundly in one's own moral wretchedness and abstain from considering both one's ability to sleep soundly and one's wretchedness in the first place. "Tell them, it's a personal matter," he says to the Receptionist. "Tell them, that I have to go out." The heads from the cubicle bank seem to rotate toward him and stare, and the Receptionist knows of course, Bloom thinks—her anemic smile and self-righteous attempt to project shame—her unresolved Electra complex and acute dysthymia—all of her ill-informed judgments and those that are perfectly justified—one never needs a full understanding of a person in order to convict.

The last time he had left work early the Receptionist brought him a bouquet of get-well carnations— it was just to make him feel guilty, Bloom thinks— treating his excuses as if they were real, when the polite thing to do, everyone knows, would be to turn a blind eye to the morally decrepit. The Reception says nothing. Standing flatfooted—time bleaches to zinc white—internally still, but continually moving outside of himself—Bloom can hear whispers of the industrial accident—descriptions of the steel mill's hoist giving way and killing nine men and two women on a Tuesday—the sound of laughter that comes from the other end

of the office—and the sound of the uninterrupt-
ed work of the Townsman and the Union Official just outside of listening distance. He imagines
their pen line scratches through the glass—vision
to sound—smell to touch—the awful things they
are writing about him and the more awful things
they are thinking but won't commit to paper—
misreporting and misremembering their dreams.

Bloom turns and strides quickly to the entry to
descend in the elevator. He travels through the
lobby and past the security check—the one-way
buffer allowing them to bring their private violence home, so long as it stays there and out of
the workplace. It is a controlled fall. The whir of
the elevator governor and tension in the wires
suspending the internal cage—stopping gently at
the lobby floor rather than dropping at terminal
velocity to the concrete below—at least this time,
Bloom thinks. There is a stillness to the outside
air. The clouds drift apart, and the ever-vacillating
cirrus fails to form neat owls or gallows or black
spots in the sky. Bloom is afraid—of aging, of nar-
rative, of the person he has become and the im-
possibility at this point of changing it—water, fate,
the kinds of people who fall asleep quickly and
those who burn in the lean hours of night, how
all of his internal neuroses transform his day-to-

day existence into a compounding paralysis—sick
but not sick enough—to be prescribed some healing salve to rub on his skin, or inert sugar pill, to
at least provide a convincing lie that would claim
to solve or mask or postpone his ills indefinitely.

He regrets taking his leave of Clytie this morning.
For not saying goodbye backed by the full charge
and presence of their shared selves. He regrets
pounding on the steering column in anger, certain
that even unexpressed thoughts, like prayer for
the better, can sabotage the present. How the rate
of forgetting a memory is steepest right after the
event. It levels off afterwards—for those unstable
impressions, not an even half-life receding, but a
pointed rate of change—like the alchemy of turning steel into gold or releasing carcinogens freely
into the air—even once it is forgotten the imprint
remains waiting to be relearned faster the second
time or taken down another fork in the mind to be
misremembered and set to another use—dragging
things out because it causes more pain that way.
Through their twelve years together Bloom has de-
veloped a fear of not running away—that feigning
death is an instinct—to blink, faint, seize with all of
his muscles at once—to hold one's breath and stick
close to the farmhouse—making sure to keep one
hand on the wall at all times—held there as if by the

instinct of some evolutionary ancestor long dead—
afraid that the predators overhead are watching.

*

Clytie jumps the crack of light that shines between the deck and the elevator cage. The space
between descends all the way to the founda-
tion—and perhaps in the time that it would take
to hit bottom she could finally picture Bloom's
face—whether coerced by necessity or failing to
react—to recognize a friend in the crowd—they
began as strangers but never believed that they
would end the same way—deferring instead to
some false impression that she has been told or
one that she has told herself—that despite or
perhaps because of her best efforts, he has trans-
formed into some off-white silhouette and that
the more that she knows the less she is able to
understand—a shadow or mirror or uncanny im-
possibility—poised like a sentinel just waiting for
his watchword to strike—but not knowing what
that watchword is, Clytie can only remain silent—
afraid to set him off and afraid to say nothing—
to move without hesitation deeper into the grid.

No one takes any notice of you so long as you
express great confidence, Clytie thinks—moving

past the reception desk parallel to the planes of glass that break in vertical lines across her mirrored reflection—the Berber carpet and fields of columns—wool suits and white button-down starched shirts—scarves and handkerchiefs and pale blue blazers. From the front, a man she passes wears the face of a Doberman Pinscher—his thin angular nose and flagstone chin—his forehead and cheeks triangle down to a single point—for better or worse, the same face he was born with, Clytie supposes—although his reflection from behind is not that of a Doberman at all, but some agreeable spaniel that greets either side of paradox with equal unconditional love. The man's reflection overlays the neighboring high rise's distant backdrop—to jump forward over the gap with Meridian nine stories below—the serious blues of Indianapolis and streaks of internal reflected white—each stacked layer of the reflection, flattened upon a single picture plane—positive and mirrored negative—and only by some optical illusion is there any depth to the inside room.

The office is lit by squares within the ceiling tiles the color of fusion. The white styrofoam drop panels are pocketed with recessed blacks—constellations or free floating stars, or dark matter absorbing sound and time—to busy oneself connecting dots and to receive one's horoscope in return, Clytie thinks—staring up at the ceiling to find out what kind of person you are. She sits at a vacant cubicle and faces Bloom's empty office—looking up to Orion and Canis Minor—down at her feet—the carpet, the Berber loops, the conspicuous lack of dust and skin cells vacuumed up every night by a wholly different set of workers—breathing and marking time with the second hand fixed to the same path and same pivot point as the day before. She torques her face to attention and focuses upon the void—the office—the appearance of being focused—typing out lightly on her borrowed keyboard: *nine men and two women are dead.*

His co-workers move as if in slow motion. Their legs drag upon each up-step, as if peeling their own skin from bone—the inert rubber of their soles from the carpet weave—as their shoulders and arms shift and swing with the pendulum recoil of what can be controlled but is easier not resisting. They are quicker to the down-step, falling with the full force of gravity that holds them in place—the magnetic pull and attraction of masses upon masses—tiny electric bonds and frictional forces that are always present but negligible—no longer negligible, Clytie thinks.

In Indianapolis they dress in theater costumes as
if for a passion play. They carry hatchets underneath their blazers prepared for their decent into
the Bronze Age just in case the modern world
gives them up—to be called upon at any moment to strike anywhere from zero to twenty-two
blows. The woman at the cubicle adjacent to where
Clytie is hiding takes a long sip from her mug
and laughs with each thin inscrutable gasping
for air—the man with the Doberman face shifts
in his seat—unable to get comfortable—unable
to sit for nine hours a day and bend himself into
L-shape after L-shape after having spent the last
millennia striving just to stand upright—looking around the office for a suitable hook to end it
all. The width of his brow indicates a disposition
towards murder, duplicity, dullness, a speed for
providing unsolicited advice and rapacious appe-
tite for self-congratulations—the woman—kindness, stoicism, wrath, a Sisyphean self-flagellation
for trying to unlearn all of the half-knowledge
that she has acquired by accident—and Clytie is
afraid to apply the same criteria to her own face.

In one of the corner offices where glass meets
glass, a middle-aged man looks out from his desk
upon the city. He wears rolled-up shirtsleeves and
a navy vest with short-cropped blond hair and

shadows underneath his chin and the recesses of his cheeks. Like an ill-fitting jigsaw, his hands are colored with intermittent thin and thick lines of blurred gray and white—pink, blue, and ochre—the crossed and juxtaposed strokes reveal all of the cracks and pores of his skin—the path and depth of each healed burn and the lithe tendons and veins beneath his surface—the horrid knuckling of his joints frozen in wretched rigor mortis, as if he is griping another's hand—but he is in fact grasping only at air—a still life of light reflected—water, smoke, wide dead fish eyes.

The windows in the office are clear to the point of invisibility. The apertures in the wall, as if open to the outside air, frame the neighboring towers. Each anonymous high rise is backdropped by another, and each false front hides its own internal skeleton. The man in the office is framed in profile against a blank white wall. He could be anywhere, Clytie thinks—working or not working—alone or with others—as if it were 1929 and he is preparing to jump, she thinks—May 8, 1945 and deciding to marry and have children—only to jump later—or to intend to but put it off indefinitely—to celebrate any number of memories or non-events—when what is noteworthy in a day is more often than not summed up in a single line—to hold on to it,

Clytie thinks—or to break down and cry for no other reason than an acute feeling of the present.

Her eyes are pulled without warning from one corner of the office to the other, and there she sees him—at least it looks like Bloom, Clytie thinks—as far as he looks like anyone. Like it had been along the canal front, she is unable to see the direction he is looking—and absent the girl on the far shore, it is impossible to know whether or not he has already seen her or is already reeling her in. With each stalking, mad, giant step upon the ground, his shoes roll along their outside edges so as to hold his head perfectly still as he pans across the plane of her vision. Every would-be stray thread and loose fiber is held in perfect alignment to the next—his hem and cuff and every pinstriped line—as if it were again 1945 and all of the naval service men are out on parade in their bleached white uniforms—as if he were acting out some mythic retelling or psychoanalytic drive that is no more or less true than any other, Clytie thinks—but at least is easier to understand in that it risks providing an answer. He holds the telephone to his ear. The Receptionist mirrors his face that Clytie cannot see for herself, and she reads Bloom by reading the Receptionist's reactions—nodding to what he is saying and revealing *nothing*—pursing her lips together to show either *concern* or *moral distaste*—or the *self-consciousness* that struck Clytie sitting upright in bed that morning—her arms resting over her knees in her gown—her bare legs and hair in a bun—looking out upon the city, not actually looking—but peering as far out onto the horizon line as she could in order to try to see inward—and as if the city were looking back, the bedroom window had framed her in full and cast its navy shadow against the blanket's lighter blue—blue washed to white in the full sun.

The Receptionist does not face Bloom directly but angles her gaze just past his eyes as if firing a warning shot across a ship's bow. Lost in the thoughts of her own violence, Clytie thinks—she fears for the Receptionist—so close to him at the mouth of his office, not four quick steps from martyrdom—so close to the end and a noble end too—full of self-sacrifice and faith—blind signifiers built up slowly from historical accounts based upon fictional accounts—rumors and unscrupulous pendants stating with the utmost certainty what is *true* or *forgotten* or *false*, and what has accrued from their collective shared absence. If she knows what is good for her, Clytie thinks—the Receptionist will recite her Act of Contrition, the *Miserere Mei*, or take on her own

ascetic conversion and fortify her own worth
through strict self-denial. Clytie wishes she could
save the Receptionist somehow but knows that
she cannot—to steal her away and begin again
to misremember—try as she might, the Receptionist's name is forgotten—escaping Clytie
even though she has met her many times—at a
holiday party with an expression of forced interest—on the street outside of a curiosity shop—
where the Receptionist had hid what she had just
purchased in a brown paper bag behind her hip.

To the Receptionist, Bloom is simply a list of
facts—his arrival and departure times—the tasks
he assigns and the phone calls received—a signa-
ture and weight and added pressure in the room—
and the return and rejection of any attempt to do
otherwise—an inability to distinguish yesterday
from today and what could possibly make tomorrow any different. There is a cant in the way
he leans upon his left leg that only a counterfeit
would form. His shoulders slant away from parallel to express his need to repent, Clytie thinks—always inventing new techniques in order to do the
same task slightly worse than the previous meth-
od—to sabotage oneself in the most complicated
fashion possible when a simple cudgel will do.

Clytie's view is cut off by the top of the cubicle wall. It frames them as if they are animate busts severed at the shoulders—a pair of disembodied heads that speak and react and pantomime at mutual respect for politeness's sake. She is unable to hear what they are saying but can smell the disinfecting scent of plastic and aerosol—of whomever was on the other line of the telephone—and the mirrored effect that Bloom has upon the Receptionist—the noxious vapors of abject terror. Clytie waits for him to reach out and swallow the Receptionist whole—to melt to the ground in a puddle of ink or yield to the whispers and echoes of the industrial accident—the rev and whining organ sustain of the overhead lights. The atmosphere in the office turns numb. Clytie seizes in her spine and shoulders—and just as abruptly as he had come into view, Bloom turns and rushes back out into the hall—disappearing into the elevator—and with the doors closing—the reflection of the inside room.

Clytie stares at herself looking before turning away. The Receptionist's pupils dilate—whether out of fear or pleasure—lowering her brow and curling the corners of her mouth back to baseline—her shoulders tighten as she takes a full step backwards—inept or bedeviled—complicit or unaware—wondering whether she is to remain unnamed or to wait patiently to be defined by another. Clytie feels that they should have lots in common considering that they share a common enemy— to have never been able to unlearn their mutual discomfort with silence—to have never failed to systematize and divide in order to find a false justification for what is beyond their control. It is not an irrational fear the Receptionist is feeling, Clytie thinks—one easily washed away as not actually being real—to be crazy and not maladjusted—to suffer from hallucinations and not illusions—but a raw recognition of the present or its absences—and in trying to hide from a face that refuses to turn towards her—Clytie lowers herself back behind the cubicle wall—she would be terrified if it did.

*

Indianapolis is a gothic city—obstinate, generous, savage, changeful—bathed in blues and yellows, whites and grays—rigid, redundant, mongrel, rude. Meridian sounds in its live clicks and diphthongs—the wavelengths just outside of Bloom's hearing—those unfiltered and made meaningless and those of the throat's first opening promise— deadened or spoken over or absorbed into the concrete and air—the walnut shells on the floor of the pit that have been thrown there haphazardly by groundlings. The street sounds tell him distinctly just how insignificant it all is, Bloom thinks—the picking of scabs and cycling through his sedating and anesthetizing thoughts—the mandatory guilt and smokescreen of his repressions—how the nurse Lola is expecting him and how in Indianapolis choosing sanity over madness is just the same as not making any decision at all—with the sun overhead at midday, the heat beats down upon his forehead and shoulders and the sidewalk white.

He lengthens his stride and pushes his pace along the walk. Within the cascade of the infinite strips of hardscape, the dividing line between each concrete pad valleys in soft horseshoed seams at each break—filling with sand and dirt—blood and sugar—pale traces of thought that jump from the sidewalk as the flat bits of quartz in the aggregate catch the overhead sun in sparks like a line of breadcrumbs to be followed. It lasts only a fraction of a moment—only so long as the mirrored surface aligns with his downward gaze—the angle of the sun and angle of Bloom's sightline—the reflection switches off in his very next stride as his eyes pass to catch the next glint of light further and further out upon the ground—a message encoded in dots and dashes, he thinks—and a jetliner thousands of feet in the air paints a single streak of white across the sky—ice melting to water and absorbed back into the air—erased.

Bloom can make out the shape of a monk, a devil, an amorphous nothing in the clouds. With the sun overhead, a crack in the sidewalk catches the toe of Bloom's wingtip and brings him to the ground hard—faster than thought—faster than feeling—his palm bracing against the sandpapered surface tears in blood smears upon the walk. The skin is scraped away and the pain comes on afterwards. It is the kind of pain that confirms one's doubts of a defendant's guilt when thirsting for a conviction, Bloom thinks—it is the kind of pain marked by cowardice and devoid of suffering—and he smiles—quite pleased with the fall—the skin, the blood, the physical evidence of the patently unjust—finding at least one justification, and one after the fact, for his complacence, passivity, indifference, anger, Bloom thinks—to reason away, if not absolve, any number of personal faults—or to soak and marinate in his particular minor aches so that the nurse Lola might pity him and Clytie won't ask any questions—how she'll tell him softly—"Everything will be alright."

If it had happened more slowly, Bloom thinks—the crowd on the sidewalk would have laughed—

suspended frame to frame—they could watch each instinctual turn and facial distortion—the plastic animal shock of descending to the ground—made ridicules without having any choice in the matter. If he were a child rather, they would call it an education—some communal rite to justify this-or-that violence—to swarm and posture and declare war—so long as it is a war they can win—with greater than three to one odds and driven by principles of overwhelming force—stepping around his body on the sidewalk like a puddle to be avoided.

Bloom's palm bleeds red like that of the traffic signal, and he takes it as a sign that the world is telling him to stop—that he is being punished for some past or future transgression or being shielded and protected from some even greater harm by being detained on sidewalk bleeding—the industrial accident—an emotional purgatory—the fact that he is fit for his particular time and place in Indianapolis—or perhaps that it means nothing at all—and he wonders whether or not that matters—the pain in his hand—his universal dismissal.

Close to the ground, the city sounds differently. He listens to its pre-lingual pulses of paired footsteps and knows without ever needing to be told that a particular set of footsteps is coming for him. Marked with the same irregular rhythm as his heartbeat—it reminds him that he is indeed still alive, because Bloom cannot trust himself to know that already—he is unable to separate the raw sound from his self-reflexive thoughts upon it—the ways in which they are coming for him and the ways in which they are indifferent to his very existence. Pure sensation is impossible, Bloom thinks—winding its way across the separate hemispheres of the mind—he is never able to leave his burning fingers in the flame just to feel them burning—to receive the impulse directly—to consider all of the sounds and heights and isolations that induce fear—the sea, the dark, the supernatural that cannot be understood, and the real which supposedly can—without feeling the overwhelming subsequent panic.

Pair after pair of brown leather shoes cross Bloom's plane of vision from the ground. They move past him unadulterated or pause but refuse to stop—taking a wider berth around his limp body on the deck—and the rhythm that is coming for him grows ever louder in its approach—the pulse increasing—feeling his own ignorance—if only he could stay blind to it, Bloom thinks—or to put it off indefinitely and never transcribe his senses into words like the Townsman—to leave the gaps in his own history of feeling free from the volumes of description and points of fact—as if they amounted to anything anyway, Bloom thinks—and how he is far too busy avoiding failure to actually succeed at anything of substance.

As a shadow breaks over him, it eases the strain on his eyes and the undertow of light bouncing off of the walk. A panhandler standing over Bloom holds up a sign asking for empathy. Blocking out the sun like an eclipse, his face is illegible. The panhandler has enormous hands—good for killing, Bloom thinks—and moving in close at an uneven 3/3 time—Bloom has located the source of his sound. He will never be my friend, Bloom thinks—with more awareness and more fortitude than himself, it is as if the panhandler can know and feel more than himself just by virtue of being a panhandler—plotting his virtuous golden mean between sloth and wrathfulness—pride and lust—to be able to parse the impossible—and in one swift motion, the panhandler lifts Bloom effortlessly up from the sidewalk with his great hands and places him back upon his feet.

Bloom counts backwards from ten to calm himself and extends his bloodied palm. He pushes forward twelve dollars without thinking—a ten and two ones—but he is afraid to look the panhandler in the eye—afraid of what he might know and afraid of the depths of feeling that he cannot possibly understand. "Thank you," the panhandler says—mirroring Bloom's expression with his own—and to imagine, Bloom thinks—saying *thank you* in a way that actually means *thank you*—to force one's instincts to be non-reactive—to receive just the right amount of pain and suffering—enough to complain and tell stories, so his would-be children will know how they had it so much easier than their hypothetical father—how Clytie will accept his own false worldliness as generosity—and yet, not so much so as to bruise—not so much so as to actually feel it.

Bloom imagines instead the panhandler as a war veteran in a tickertape parade. The confetti falls as if it were May 8, 1945—a reminder to be grateful—November 7, 1952—the birth of an American hero. I prefer this war veteran to his other self, Bloom thinks—traveling home from overseas with the honest blue collar hope of working the assembly line in Gary—to vacation each winter in Bermuda shorts and smoke unabashedly around his children. He imagines the panhandler speaking with a Midwestern accent, and it sounds so much more trustworthy than the silences he receives from Lola or Clytie who do not say what they mean and who have let their own accents bleed out. The panhandler rolls his fingers and curls them under. He takes a further step forward and compresses the space between them—reaching out with his hand, Bloom cannot tell if he is making a threat or a gesture at friendship—whether he is a war veteran at all—the internal charge sparking light from the sidewalk—a magnetic resistance—and the panhandler rises to a terrible height—raising his fist before him—poised to strike or to protect him to the last—but not willing to find out, Bloom turns in the opposite direction and runs.

He jogs the length of Meridian to the parking deck without looking back. His eyes adjust to the dark and his nose and ears to the air—an entombed dirt-metal smell of oil emanates from the seepages that have dried into the concrete and sweat during the heat of the day. At the Lincoln Bloom mechanically turns the latch and starts the ignition—the embedded motion played over thousands of times without thought just as the thousands of other movements and impulses that have become habit. Winding forward through the garage, the sun flares white and breaks upon Bloom's skin and eyes as he exits onto the street—safely behind glass to look out onto the world. Each window on the avenue doubles for another. They each catch the

reflections of their opposites like sundials simultaneously fixed and in time. Bloom passes his own
building and the conference room window on the
ninth floor—his own office—wondering whether
or not they have noticed that he is gone and feeling
their indifference and his own hypocritical sadness—punishing himself in order to feel centered
or to feel their eyes upon him—watching from
above as the Lincoln advances up the avenue—
the phantom grip of their hands on his shoulder.

*

She knows that she should not leave the safety
of her hiding place. Concealed in plain view—
Clytie did not realize that she had already made
the decision long before actually stepping forward. Waiting at an open door whose curtained
stairs lead up and out of the theater, Clytie imagines—suspended in the moment on the threshold and now unable to stop herself from going
forward—wondering whether or not they are one
and the same. She looks down at the carpet in
her daydream and its swirling leaves of rich bur-
gundy. The grain catches the light at her feet—it
is the brightest point in the room—and with a
blink, turning back into the plain beige Berber
loops of the present. By forgetting how to pic-

ture paradise, she does not know what to wish for, and not knowing what to do besides step forward, she crosses the space between herself and his office—repentance and apathy—point of fact and point of feeling—Clytie travels at right angles within the grid—down to the end of the row and left, and right again, in snaking straight lines.

Looking over their desks as she passes, Clytie watches news of the accident flash across one computer screen and then another—confirming what they have heard already that *nine men and two women are dead.* They stare at their hands and screens. They sip coffee and sit with upright postures. Believing, Clytie supposes—that it is not in good taste to show any sadness below the level of soft sighing or joy above a muted good cheer—to be out of phase with expectation. The man with the Doberman face looks forward, blank and wide-eyed—the man in the corner office is either working diligently or staring out the window—and the inscrutable woman in the adjacent cubicle looks inscrutable—expressing their collective ambivalence to how sad it all seems—always to seem and never to be, Clytie thinks—but shifting their necks towards her just as she passes, she feels their eyes upon her in the pre-cognitive way of sense and suspicion—a justified mistrust and justified prejudice—the whole office stares as she walks over the threshold straight into Bloom's office.

Clytie can feel the absence of the spaces he has just left—she can feel the workers' eyes upon her and the echoes of her own wake. His desk is pushed up against the window—its oak surface, a plank to be walked upon gingerly—only a plane glass interrupts one from spilling over onto the street bottom—and Clytie focuses upon the concrete, the neighboring building, her own reflection staring back—imagining Bloom spending his working day cycling between planes and the movement across them—the dips and divisions of his thinking—looking at himself and looking down to the street—gratitude, grace, desire—to glance across to the other side of the avenue and feel another's eyes upon him. The straight-backed chair is pushed away from the desk and is canted at an angle that tells her that he left in a hurry—as if to say *you are the sixth or seventh most important person in my life*, Clytie imagines. She tries sitting so as to view the room from where he does—resting her palms on the surface of his desk—the neighboring rooftop is inundated with heating and mechanical ducts—on its facade, rows of classical columns and arched windows are spaced evenly across its front—and down on Meridian Bloom is running away.

She tries to remember the day they met. A summer evening—enclosed on the porch and unable to see past the radius of a single luminous bulb—the white board and batten walls and curtained windows shield the black depth inside of the house. They lean on the railing together—Bloom facing her directs his gaze down to the crack at the base of the door—Clytie leaning straight legged in ballet flats looks out onto what may or may not be hiding behind a shadow—their cutout eyes matching one-to-one with the inky night behind them. The astral hues above their heads promising a midday sky is in fact an illusion. She tries to remember the sense of attraction she must have felt—to remember other days in images and fractions of images—colors, sounds—a white and green gingham dress or the morphing alkaline shade of a hydrangea—the passing off of silence for knowledge and fear for prudent self-restraint. It is a revisionist history to pretend to have had what was never there in the first place. It is nothing at all like what it was or should have been, Clytie thinks—and how it might have possibly been recorded and remembered if it were.

In war there are bound to be casualties. She looks at his desk for signs—not in any direct sense, Clytie thinks—but for that which might point to another—always one step removed—and not necessarily moving toward what truly may be in the strict sense, but the story she wants to be told and the one to tell herself—based upon but not committed to truth—a love story—but what is that anyway but Stockholm or Stendhal syndromes moving the beholder to yield. She examines in turn the scraps of illegible handwriting canted at hard angles that she cannot read. She picks up a note written to Bloom in her own hand that she does not remember writing—wishing him—*the best of luck*—with his mistrust of all people, Clytie thinks—with his holding on to the illusion of doing something useful—and how impersonal it seems—*the best of luck*—as if she were providing Bloom forewarning of her own following—forewarning for how she might paint him if she could—in short fits and starts of dappled blues and streaked yellows—a portrait in profile—where off to one side she would place a window that opens up onto the city cut by the outside edge of the canvas—the frame incomplete and the window running outside the limits of its own boarders. This is how she knows the world doesn't stop, Clytie tells herself.

She has felt this feeling before, she thinks—believing for a moment that everything would come out just this way and she would find herself alone with every errant thought negated before it can ever take root—node resting next to antinode and held there—seeing things for what they are and not what they want to be or could potentially become—ungenerous facts trumped by absolutes—wishing she could believe otherwise and to have faith in some alternative prime mover that wasn't always so grave. In a dream once, she had followed a child over a rise at the edge of a wood. Between the trees, where Clytie believes she might be buried, a light fades quickly to black against a radiant lawn, and the child waves her forward—not knowing who is truly leading who and not knowing how to tell the difference, both wondering where they are being taken, they feign smiles and try to hold the other's weight.

Clytie can hear a rush of footsteps from behind—a pulse inside her body synced to the vibration in the floor—and there must be some resonance that she cannot feel—earthquakes that go unrecorded—nonsense symbols and myths that she does not believe in—she looks down upon Bloom's desk and the grains of the wood tightening and loosening along its surface—the sun overhead and held there—feeling the weight of someone standing behind her. Uncertain about how much time has past—Clytie can feel the figure's pressure and pulse untethered in the room—a guilt wasted on herself because she has given up on caring—face down in the canal—between the oak trees—memories rewritten so that she never escapes—and a voice softly speaks from behind so as not to startle her—"Mrs. Bloom?" the Receptionist asks—"Can I help you?"

*

The street is full of white pants and brown leather shoes—western plaids, red dyed hairstreaks—and the white hospital jackets pushing gurneys without any haste. In Indiana—the humidity and constant blue-yellow haze—leather seats, traffic stop—tiny repetitive traffic loops—blue Ford Taurus after blue Ford Taurus—beige, white, fire engine red—Bloom idling his Lincoln in the hospital pick-up lane, and he waits patiently for Lola Lola to get off of her shift. In the Lincoln he feels like he is effecting change—patience, an extended timeline—where anything becomes small and ruin is contextualized—decontextualized—with a gesture and a lean to the white jackets pushing gurneys—moving the dead back and forth.

In the shadow of the hospital, a shade is cast over the crosswalk and the adjacent construction site—an accident, Bloom thinks—most things are accidents—the different degrees of manslaughter—"Manslaughter," he says to himself—just the sound of the term—more acute somehow within the shadow of the hospital and within listening distance of the construction site than inside his office—than on the street. He sees a cowboy smoking by the entry—a naval cadet—an anonymous man crying—and the crying man is not very methodical, Bloom thinks—but all over the place—undisciplined, unattractive—the sidewalk is full of hideous men.

He wishes he could subvert his own impulses—falling in love as the unsolicited giving of one's soul to destroy as the recipient sees fit—the nurse Lola's refusal to meet him on the river walk—the anonymous man's unbounded lack of self-discipline—I wish I could allow myself to weep on the street corner, Bloom thinks—to be abused and tested and considering the possibility of whether she will either destroy him or else she will not. Lola Lola smiles as she walks out of the automatic doors and towards the hospital pickup lane—compassionate, charming—like the panhandler, charming—and she approaches the Lincoln in her white hospital uniform flanked by two doctors—and I feel good about these men, Bloom thinks—to be terrified—their white jackets and white hands and white shirts—waving with smiles as she enters the Lincoln—the doctors waving as they pull away. The doctors wave and smile—white jacket—solitary gurney—ten meters—twenty—away and still smiling.

As the road recedes, she turns her head to see if the doctors are still behind them—two white figures on a field of gray. Bloom drives with the self-assertion he imagines one should—to construct his identity first and build himself to match—through one layer and the first moments of resistance—blanched paler the deeper that he digs—or cracking and breaking off into sudden unrealistic expectations or nihilistic entitlement—self-fulfilling sabotage to prove his own pity right. Has he in fact resigned himself to the blasphemous, Bloom thinks. This is what love looks like—ground to the frenzied paralysis of silence—empty resolutions to do otherwise or the continuation of stoic indifference to act out of fear when one's internal shape is blown violently open and left raw to the world. No, he tells himself. From the Lincoln, the city yields no great vistas or city lights—with no proper frontage, natural shore, or man-made central park—Indianapolis stretches the whole county so that one never knows when they have entered or when they have left. Outside of downtown—but still contained from within—in every direction it is amorphous and flexing, as if inviting what lacks clear definition to be implanted with anything—taken over and made one's own.

The nurse Lola sits in the passenger seat. She sits quietly—having spent all day in the laboratory clean room—the air in the car must seem filthy and unfit, Bloom thinks—its microbes and static and flecks of dust—things for which he does not know the names of and does not want to know— cycling and recycling through their lungs and cast back upon the leather to lie dormant for hours or days until their own bodies stir them up again— with fever and fetid breath—the vents angled down to the floor—cycling back dust into their mouths with unconscious reflexive inhales. He imagines what their life would be like together—truly awful, Bloom thinks—domesticated out of fear or bullied by exhaustion—with a beige house and an easy commute into Indianapolis—Zionsville to downtown—and Old Testament-like Zion—and Old Testament-like awful—except more beige and more affluent—absorbing all of their neighbor's cheap nocturnal aspirations as their own and ignoring without question the sensible good advice to keep your head down and hair cut short.

Lola is silent. Ever since entering the car she has stared forward with an anxious look on her face. Bloom tries to consider the cause or contributing source—the doctors or the laboratory—to be held within a sterile environment for the length of the working day and to be released into the city air—a birth in miniature repeated and replayed six days out of seven—or the imaging of radioactive dyes on circulating blood—waiting and hoping for a reaction that may or may not have any palliative effect or any side consequence—synthesizing compounds in mechanized and militaristic fashion and praying collectively for their own Salvarsan 606—with too little phlegm and too much yellow bile.

*

Clytie thinks of her namesake in Ovid falling in love with the sun. Unable to have him, she watches his daily crossings from one end of the sky to the other, fixed to a single spot on the ground longingly tracing his arc. Her limbs sprout roots and dig violently into the earth, her body hardening into the stem and bud of a sunflower. It won't do, Clytie thinks—the inertia of the day—the overhead halogen lights and soft cycling air, the same upstairs as it is down, and the thinnest of illusions that she will be able to break with her suspicion that

the Receptionist might tell her which direction
he has gone. Clytie looks hard into her face as if
something were hidden there—under the eyelids
perhaps—or between the Receptionist's lips—the
slightest of gaps—at home on the edge of her bed
with her head hung, Clytie imagines—the Receptionist's bare thighs and shoulders—the clothes
she had worn from the working day refolded and
piled on the dresser for what would be tomorrow.

The light in Bloom's office casts a rectangle onto
the ground that Clytie does not dare to cross. She
stands on the leeward side of the sun so that her
shadow does not break upon it. The Receptionist
remains still and appears to stop breathing—her
features cast in bronze or plaster. Having lost all
track of time, the minutes slip from Clytie just as
soon as they seem within her grasp—and outside
within the natural call and response of conversation,
the office workers pass without notice or crashing
to a standstill. It is as if Clytie could walk around
the office and observe them as statuary—to get up
close and see what the Receptionist might be hiding in her cheeks and jawbone—how it is somehow unreasonable to be terrified, Clytie thinks—or
that she had imagined the silences between them
in the farmhouse—and instead of following him
across the city, she might have run to some fixed

place she can count on—the embroidered couch or the corner of the living room where one white wall meets another—as if these points in space are any more stable, Clytie thinks—negating herself as soon as she is emboldened enough wish for it—her mind races and cools back to stillness—the Receptionist frozen before her pinking back to life.

A shout behind them calls Clytie back to the present. We have either lost faith in our common man or declared war, Clytie thinks. Though she notes that the Receptionist remains unmoved—alive again with her heart beating—her jaw relaxes and seems unconcerned about any imminent threat—at rest and non-reactive. Perhaps she had imagined it, Clytie thinks—the shouts behind her, the confidence she had in entering, the calling back to life of what was missing a moment before. Clytie trusts the Receptionist more than she trusts herself, she thinks—which is not to say much—but she trusts the Receptionist enough to provide a roadmap to follow and ignore through swaths of pathologic ambivalence. Behind them Clytie again hears the sound of the hive crescendo—their eyes upon her, she thinks—unable to look, but sensing their unconscious suspicion—their mistrust and judgment and animal logic—and the Receptionist's inexhaustible patience.

Clytie can see the image she holds of Bloom fold into her own reflection. She can the girl in the white dress attending to guests at her funeral—her own bemused disillusionment to be present there, Clytie thinks—with an anger that she cannot and perhaps never can let go—hypocritically begrudging what she will not commit to herself—when all she really wants is a shared sense of loss, Clytie thinks—as if that should be so difficult to find—to be bonded in mutual shared suffering. Clytie is not one to commit to utopian ideals, because they are wrong, she thinks—but always grateful to those who do, because they seem to treat her so very kindly. The Receptionist must be some kind of hard line utilitarian—"Are you alright," she asks again—"Yes, thank you," Clytie says breaking her silence—"I'm fine"—and to her own surprise—and not knowing it until the words had left her mouth—it seems to be true.

Clytie turns away from the Receptionist and towards the inner room. All appears as it had before—the man with the Doberman face typing on his computer—the inscrutable woman returning to her desk with coffee—hiding behind their cubicle walls and pretending to work or sealing themselves in the conference room. Not knowing where Bloom has gone and not wanting him to get away, she moves back over the threshold. Down the elevator, Clytie descends in slow easy suspension—to be enclosed within—faster and faster—through the lobby and past the Security Guard—and to think what might have been— each chamber echoes differently and the outside air releases the idle internal pressure. Clytie scans for Bloom's silhouette down either side of the walk. She looks past a line of protestors with open mouths and exposed teeth. A man with white pants and brown leather shoes with some near recognition to another, Clytie thinks. In the thousands of windows overlooking Meridian, if only there was someone on the other side to look down and provide her Bloom's location on the grid— to be her co-conspirator—to look him in the face and relay back his ill-temper—his helplessness—his disgust, surprise, shame, guilt, and joy.

She looks for a face she would no longer recognize, Clytie supposes—an anonymous gray suit amongst anonymous gray suits—and his perfect proportions ever radiating outward—the one person in Indianapolis who perhaps no longer casts a shadow. Clytie stops and does nothing. Pedestrians pass in both directions—cars pack in tight lines and expand in stretched speeding dashes. Passing directly in front of her—a black Lincoln drives slowly up Meridian—black and anonymous—as if trying not to call attention to itself—Bloom's silhouette carved in the driver's seat. She watches the car recede up the avenue but refuse to diminish—straight past one intersection and then another, but refusing to turn—as if Clytie could will it forward and keep it in her view—as if he were being pulled in single straight line towards the City Hospital—its gray square on a pale blue backdrop—and Clytie rushes after.

*

From the Lincoln, Indianapolis fixes its horizon line. A single point drawn across their view and broken only by the spiraling on and off ramps of the highway that spike in graded verticals before returning back to baseline. On the side of the road, the painted white line that marks the shoulder runs and weaves in subtle serpentine darts. Bloom pushes the Lincoln faster, and the line speeds alongside of them enlivened, slows, and is ultimately left for dead at a traffic light. The asphalt forms a zippered edge that bleeds into the grasses—the loose pebbles, once part of the whole, crumble forward and are pushed back—with the spaces in between that shift imperceptibly—smoothed over or filled in along the delirious seam at the edge of the highway.

Bloom keeps his eyes forward and does not dare to look at Lola sitting beside him. In the rearview, the white jackets pop in and pop out of his vision in clouds or streaks of light that spark and split into colors. Memories that refuse to recede magnify as the Lincoln pulls up the avenue—leaving the farmhouse in silence—waiting alongside the canal front—the violent swing of the high rise that bends when the wind blows without anyone noticing—the difference being inside or watching its false stillness from without—a once perfect geometry skewed on a slant in surreal art deco. The city at different scales bleeds in all directions, and whatever natural topography there might have been is cut with blades and turned over and filled in with river stone—buried pipes and electrical lines stacked on top of one another—recorded and promptly forgotten—dug up as unmarked graves in great exhales of steam and fire and slow drips into the water table.

The nurse Lola has tiny hands and near invisible keratin buds for fingernails painted a burnt red. Staring forward—Bloom waits for her to compliment his promptness, his instinct, his neat charcoal suit—to respond favorably, he thinks—

to his lies without actually believing them to be lies—but to act as if she does without placing any additional weight or responsibility upon him to actually fulfill his promises and make them true, while at the same time waiting for her to confirm her own unwavering resolve, Bloom thinks—real resolve and not the artful kind—never to be one for double standards and never to be one that is unpatriotic—he wonders when Lola might tell him where she might like to go—and he wonders what untruths the Charge Nurse may have told her and what false assumptions she might be basing her own false assumptions upon.

He extends his hand and shows her the hardened blood and loose gravel on the underside of his palm. Its once red turned to near black—he tells her how he was assaulted by pair of army officers who threw him rudely to the ground—each one a war hero—and how it is not normally in their characters to throw strangers to the ground, Bloom explains—but how he forgave them afterwards given that they were army officers and war heroes after all. He torques his voice and says nothing of the panhandler or the sidewalk crack—nothing of being left alone on the canal front—and still she continues to ignore him and stare out the window. Unmoved and unaf-

fected—it is as if she isn't grateful at all, Bloom
thinks—isn't listening to his story—and he can
feel his pulse rising—he can feel the traffic din—
never to scratch an itch directly but the skin just
beside it—he tears at himself in and around each
emerging thought and each alternative timeline.

They pass a street that in all likelihood has a name,
but Bloom is unable to find a street sign and confirm his position on the grid. Unable to confirm
where he might find a comfortable cozy back al-
ley to be murdered in, Bloom thinks. When his
greatest accomplishment is failing to voice his own
ignorance and to pretend like it never existed, or to
imagine whatever fantasy and work under the as-
sumption that it is real. Today is good day to yield
passively to self-hate, Bloom tells himself. Today is
a good day to abandon one's principles of self-de-
termination and faith in his fellow man. Bloom
squeezes his fingers around the steering column—
the radio dial is switched off—the grooves in the
upholstery valley at tight seams—and the air is
taken in from the outside and cycled through the
filter, his lungs, his coursing veins and capillaries.

The Lincoln slows and the traffic seems to come
from their front, bottling the road to a standstill.
In an adjacent car, a man listening to music ap-

pears held in a state of joy and forgetfulness. In a white pickup, a couple smiles at one another seemingly without malevolence. The driver's side window frames the city. With the sun sitting directly overhead, the War Memorial is backdropped against the sky. The marble's white takes on the colors that surround it—imprinted and indelibly marked, Bloom thinks—the sun's canary-yellow—white washed to gray and white again.

*

Inside the hospital, Clytie walks down a hallway wide enough for two gurneys. Squares of linoleum reflect the banded strips of light overhead, and rows of evenly spaced red doors lead the way forward—red squares on a field of yellow—the cinderblock walls return back to center each echo and each first opening of sound—magnified or diminished—every electric beep and exhale and declaration of love, Clytie thinks—she scans the faces of those in street clothes first and the nurses and doctors afterward—a pair of orderlies and a man exiting the hospital with his spaniel—the smell of antiseptic and cologne convincing her that they are all to one degree or another hiding something—decay or death or unseen desire— with the automatic doors opening and closing of their own accord—it cuts the cries of the outside air—on to off—embraced and hushed to silence.

The lines of the hallway appear to expand and compress in from their sides. The path forward turns and turns in upon itself—circling so as never to end, Clytie thinks—with fault lines concealed below all the layers of paint making promises of future collapse—one day or another—if not now, then certainly soon. She listens to her heart beat and the even inhale and exhale of her breath—the anxiety, fear, sudden onset fatigue, or mania—the overheard heart monitor in an adjacent room and the low crying vowel sounds of either pain or joy, but she is unable to tell which—Clytie moves down the hallway and catches nondescript washes of blurred gray that sharpen in her periphery to absolute fidelity but fade when she turns to face them directly—a charcoal suit shifting to blue—a face washed of all color filled with flashes of life and heat.

I am perfectly at ease, Clytie tells herself—and if only she could trick her body into believing as much. Her heels sound in low clicks off of the tile and return back to her ears in stereo—doubled over or halved—the hall fills and then empties to nothing. Tides of patients are wheeled forward and wheeled back, and time slows and speeds ahead with the utmost of urgency. Passing exam room after exam room, Clytie looks inside at each intersection to find him, to find the other, to confirm what she knows already, or to catch in fragments what she finds impossible to see in full. Inside—a silver-haired woman asleep and dreaming—a couple staring transfixed at an all but silent television—Marlene Dietrich dancing in a cabaret—the swollen purpled feet and blanched patches of skin on bare shoulders—and a cry of pain that Clytie identifies as pain—not one from any external pressure, she thinks, but a breach or failure from inside.

Along the corridor, the spaces recede into their own private depths. It is a different temperature and color and time of day inside than it is out, and it is different further within each room. In the operating theater—a nurse poised with a syringe in hand on the verge of sticking a sleeping patient. In another—a man very much awake braces for his own needle—feeling the pinprick beforehand and distorting his face like some primal dog. Behind glass—the backlit display of a patient's insides, holding out the hope for recovery or revenge. The hallway turns and turns again. In a laboratory—a light from the base of a microscope courses up through its slide and blood and coverslip—to see inside another, Clytie thinks—gray suit after gray suit—but it is never Bloom—and he must have slipped past her—or turned the other way.

Clytie sits on a hard plastic bench designed to prevent the homeless from sleeping. There is a rhythm to the hospital that she cannot observe directly and a pull on the overhead lights that make it bend in an arc that curves unnaturally past her eyes. Her feet dangle and fall heavy to the tile—moving one foot and then the other—Clytie wiggles her toes inside of her shoes. Lifting herself again, she stands and begins walking—stops, breathes—watches the light off of the red doors and yellow walls—bending—and steps forward again.

Many thanks to all of those who helped make this book possible. Especially to François Camoin, Karen Brennan, Paisley Rekdal, Scott Black, Ed Pavlić, Judith Ortiz Cofer, Andrew Zawacki, Rachel Hanson, Nate Liederbach, Michelle Kyoko Crowson, Davis Schneiderman, Rachel Tenuta, and all of Lake Forest College Press. To the English Departments at the University of Utah and the University of Georgia, thank you. Thank you Johnny Damm, Bradley Bazzle, Will Dunlap, and Lindsey Harding. Thank you to *1913: a journal of forms* where an earlier version of an excerpt first appeared. To Josh Corey for your kind attention to the manuscript, thank you. Thank you Madeleine Plonsker for your generosity and foresight without which this would not be possible. Thank you Anne-Laure Tissut for selecting the book and the friendship since. Deepest gratitude to Elizabeth Cunningham, thank you for everything. To Mom, Dad, Michael, David, Liz, Willow, Brad, and Alexander, I can't thank you enough.

THE PLONSKER SERIES

Each year Lake Forest College Press / &NOW Books awards the Madeleine P. Plonsker Emerging Writers Residency Prize to a poet or fiction writer under the age of forty who has yet to publish a first book. The winning writer receives $10,000, three weeks in residency on the campus of Lake Forest College, and publication of his or her book by Lake Forest College Press / &NOW Books, with distribution by Northwestern University Press.

Past winners:

- Jessica Savitz, *Hunting Is Painting* (poetry)
- Gretchen Henderson, *Galerie de Difformité* (fiction)
- Jose Perez Beduya, *Throng* (poetry)
- Elizabeth Gentry, *Housebound* (fiction)
- Cecilia K. Corrigan, *Titanic* (poetry)

For more information about the Plonsker Prize and how to apply, visit